Her Miracle Cowboy

Texas Knights, Volume 3

Janalyn Knight

Published by Janalyn Knight, 2021.

Chapter One

Acacia Richards finished cleaning Bobby up and fastened his clothing. It had been all she could do to drag herself out of bed this morning, and now she had only minutes until her twin brother's new physical therapist arrived. She lowered him from the bed and settled him into his wheelchair. Morning sunlight shone bright through the open curtains on Bobby's dark-blond hair.

She closed her eyes. *God, I can't do this anymore. Please, I just can't.* Hot tears pooled behind her eyelids. But tears were useless. She'd learned that a long time ago. A moment later, the doorbell rang. Slowly her eyes opened, and she blinked them dry.

Bobby grinned.

The corner of her mouth tilted up, and she wheeled him into the living room, stopping the chair in front of the TV where his cartoons played.

Still wearing the leggings and T-shirt she'd slept in, she hadn't even brushed her hair before wadding it up and clipping it behind her head. She didn't need a mirror to know that the usual circles under her eyes would be dark from lack of sleep. Cursed as she was with a porcelain doll's skin, the slightest blemish showed clearly.

When she opened the door, instant heat crawled toward her cheeks. Instead of a woman like Marilyn, their previous PT, she faced a tall, rocking-hot guy in a scrub top and Wranglers pressed so stiff they'd stand on their own. A crisp, fresh cologne wafted past her nose.

His light-brown eyes twinkled, surely at her dumbstruck expression.

"C-come in. Sorry, I got up late. I mean, we're ready now. But just barely," she stammered, like an idiot. Had Marilyn said her replacement was a man? How had she missed that? His shirt stretched over his chest and upper arms, and his jeans hugged his narrow hips. Acacia couldn't help but stare. His body was raw, sculpted muscle. He was by far the finest male specimen she'd laid eyes on in a while. She took a deep breath and backed away from the door.

He grinned as he entered the room and offered his hand. "Hi, I'm Noah Rowden. If you need more time, please, go ahead."

Her girly brain screamed at her to run for the sanctuary of the bedroom to repair her appearance. Instead, she shook his hand, a tight smile on her face, and walked into the living room. Turning Bobby's wheelchair around, she patted his shoulders. "This is Noah. He'll help you like Marilyn did. Noah, meet my brother, Bobby."

The therapist bent down and shook her brother's hand, saying, "May I give you something?"

Bobby grinned crookedly. "Uh-huh."

Noah wrapped his arms around her brother's broad shoulders and squeezed him in a gentle hug. "That was from Marilyn. She told me what a hard worker you are and said she misses you."

Still smiling, Bobby said, "Marilyn. I love Marilyn," in his slightly slurred voice.

Noah knelt on the floor. "She loves you too." Unzipping his therapy bag, he pulled out a file folder.

Acacia knew what it would say. Her brother had amnesia, the cognitive functioning of a four-year-old, and was quadriplegic. Thank you, Afghanistan.

After making a quick note, Noah returned the folder to his bag and searched inside again, finally bringing out a large red toy car with a raised yellow button on top. "I brought you something to play with."

Her brother laughed, and his arms made small spastic movements while his blue eyes focused on the car.

Noah pushed the button, and a loud siren sound wailed through the room while the headlights flashed on and off.

Her brother threw his head back and shrieked his laughter. "I wa-a-ant it. Can I ha-a-ave it?" High emotion made his speech less clear.

"Of course. I'll teach you how to push the button. You have to work hard. I'll leave it here so you can practice." He placed the car in Bobby's lap and helped him move his forearm to the yellow button. The siren filled the room, and Bobby laughed. No matter how many times he succeeded, he never failed to howl with joy.

After a time, the therapy moved to lower body exercises. With the help of the Hoyer lift, Acacia and Noah lowered her brother to a soft blanket on the carpet. Noah worked Bobby's legs one at a time, increasing his flexibility and using every muscle.

Most of the movements were familiar to Acacia, as she did therapy with her brother every morning on the days he didn't have a PT visit.

Noah's shoulder muscles bunched and released, stretching the fabric of his scrub top as he moved Bobby's legs. His long, supple back arched, and she imagined him naked, hovering above her bare breasts. She snapped her head up. *God!* Where in the hell had that come from?

Hopping off the couch, she strode into the kitchen for another cup of coffee. So it was true. After two years, she was desperate, lusting after the first male trapped in her presence. Leaning on the cabinet, she buried her face in her hands. The emptiness she lived with, day in and day out, overwhelmed her. After several moments, she gathered her courage. She was stronger than this. Strong enough to face this man. To face another day—alone.

Acacia reentered the living room as the session wrapped up, and she helped Noah put her brother in the lift, then back into his wheelchair.

Bobby was once a big man at six feet two inches and two hundred pounds. Now he weighed less with muscle loss but was still quite a handful.

A nurse's aide from the Veterans Affairs Department assisted Acacia with Bobby's bath three days a week. One day each week, she had a VA caregiver who stayed a short time with him while she ran errands and bought groceries. The rest of the time she was alone with him. This brought back the crushing weight she'd awakened with, and a deep sigh escaped her.

Noah raised a brow. "You okay?"

She spun away from him. How could she feel this way? Her brother was so vulnerable—so helpless. What kind of sister was she to dream of escape? Of a new life? A life without this responsibility? Hot blood rose up her neck. What would this man think of her if he knew she yearned to get away from this house—away from the weight that nearly knocked her to her knees on her bad days? She mumbled, "Uh, yeah. I'm fine."

"Acacia?

Still facing away, she said, "The car is a great idea. I can see where, over time, it may help Bobby gain more control over his arms. He certainly loves it. You're the first one to see him as I do—as a little boy who wants to have fun. That's really who he is now."

"I gathered that from the notes in his file. I like to motivate my patients with fun things because so much of what I do is boring or hard work."

She turned back, her face now under control. "Thank you. I'm sure you'll be good for my brother."

Later that morning, after feeding Bobby the breakfast he'd missed, Acacia retreated to the back porch, her safe place, where she had her container garden. The exquisite taste of a sun-ripened tomato, the crisp pop as she crunched into a fresh jalapeno pepper, or cooking with her home-grown herbs were her greatest pleasures.

Some of the morning's tension eased. What had come over her when Noah was here? That sex fantasy was some kind of crazy. The last two grueling years had worn her strong resolve to care for her twin down to a ragged thing. She hardly recognized herself anymore. Physically she was thinner, honed to a strange, harder replica of herself. Emotionally, she was strung out, tuned to a raw edge.

But the worst part, what had become increasingly hard to bear, was the isolation. The four walls of her home had been closing in on her the past few months. The people she was close to were back in Howelton, in North Texas. While caring for her brother, she had no avenue to meet new people, to go out and blow off steam. Bone-deep, she felt the lack of friends, of family surrounding her. Though her best friend, Sarah, came as often as possible, her visits just weren't enough. Way down at the bottom of Acacia's soul there was a big, black nothing where Johnny used to be. Loving him back then, before Bobby, had filled her to the brim.

She missed it terribly. Romance. Having a man's strong arms around her. Adoring everything about Johnny and planning her dream wedding with her friends. This was her darkest secret. How ugly was this need of hers when her poor brother had lost his body, his soul, serving his country? Everything that was Bobby had been blown up on a battlefield in Afghanistan. And little Acacia wanted romance? She couldn't stomach herself sometimes.

After setting her now-empty iced-tea glass down on the table, she grabbed her gardening basket and shears. The spicy smells of her pepper and tomato plants called to her. Pruning and harvesting her vegetable garden was one of her most treasured joys. She chewed her lower lip. Noah had said he'd see her brother on Tuesdays and Thursdays. That gave her two days to get herself under control.

* * *

Noah grabbed a bag of feed from the flatbed trailer and stacked it in the barn. Ronnie, his best friend and roping partner, was right behind him with another sack. They'd just gotten home from Jupe Mills in Fredericksburg, where they'd bought horse and cattle feed at bulk price. The ranch had been in Noah's family for three generations. As the only healthy male heir in the family, he was incredibly lucky to have inherited it.

Ronnie reached out, stopping his friend before he grabbed his next bag. "What about this new client you mentioned?"

"He's a cool guy. An Afghanistan veteran. Came back a mess. His sister's taking care of him. Thing is, he's like a young child now—has severe intellectual disabilities. Acacia, his sister, is wonderful. Been caring for him two years."

"What's she look like? I can see you like her."

Noah took his hat off and squeezed the brim, wiping sweat from his brow. "Well, she's a looker, all right. But she's worn down. Life hasn't been easy on her. Her hair's real dark, and her skin's pale. Looks like you might blow her over with a feather. Makes a man want to take care of her, you know? Something about the eyes." He put on his hat. "She's tough, though. I got that too."

He hadn't been able to quit thinking about her. With her hair pulled back in a simple clip, she had a wholesome, sexy look, though her solemn expression made her seem sad. And her lips—they were just full enough to be tempting without detracting from her overall air of sweetness.

Ronnie raised a brow. "Sounds like you're into her."

Noah headed over to pick up another sack, breathing in a hint of the sweet feed inside. "Not sure what I can do about it, if I am."

Ronnie followed him, not giving up. "Well, you said your client's like a child, right?"

"Yep."

"She could use a man in her life, you ask me."

Noah turned, hands on his hips. "I'm not asking you, all right? I can't do something like that. I'm Bobby's therapist. It wouldn't be right."

Ronnie stood his ground. "I say you can. She's not your client, he is. Two years have passed. Is he getting any better?"

"No."

"There you go. You said she's worn down. She needs support. Anyone would. Look at the responsibility she's taken on. Hell, she needs somebody—something—more than what's she got looking her in the face right now."

Noah picked up a bag of feed and walked into the barn.

Ronnie followed with another sack. "Well?"

Noah shook his head. "Well, dammit, nothing's ever easy."

"Nope."

Noah gusted out a breath. Bobby was part of the problem. He reminded him of Joe. His older brother had suffered a traumatic brain injury when he was five years old while mutton busting at a local rodeo. The sheep he was riding ran him head-on into a steel pipe fence post. Back then, kids didn't wear helmets. After weeks in a coma, Joe had awakened, but he'd never talked, walked, or cared for himself again.

The guilt of being the son who could run, laugh and play had never left Noah. Watching the physical therapists work tirelessly with Joe's lifeless arms and legs had inspired Noah in his vocation. He wanted to make a difference in his patients' lives. And he did. Well, most of the time. But the cases like Joe's, and maybe Bobby's, broke his heart. Many times, his job was holding back the tide of muscle deterioration, not improving a patient's condition.

He had hope for Bobby, though. There was a chance that he might increase his arm control. Noah would give it everything he had for that chance.

* * *

Acacia had spent most of Bobby's PT visit this morning cleaning the house in any place but the living room, making sure more fantasies about Noah were out of the question. She'd learned firsthand how a man felt about a woman with a responsibility like Bobby in her life.

By early afternoon, she turned off the faucet and placed the final dirty bowl in the dishwasher, the smell of bleach telling her the kitchen was clean. If she kept going like this, her house would be spotless.

Her cell rang, and she dried her hands as she walked to the table to answer it. *Sarah.* Acacia sighed and considered letting the call go to voicemail. She wasn't up to being grilled by her best friend. Snatching the phone before it rang for the last time, she put on a cheery voice. "Hi. What's up?"

"Does something have to be up for me to check in with my bestie? How are you, honey? How are you holding up?"

Always the same old question. "I'm doing fine."

"Have you found a sitter yet? Did you run an ad or check for an agency? You know I'll pay for it."

Acacia held the phone against her chest and closed her eyes. Why couldn't Sarah leave it alone? Her friend meant well, but Acacia couldn't let any old stranger stay with Bobby. Her brother wasn't a child, and despite his size, his health was fragile. Even with the excellent care she provided, urinary tract infections were a constant threat. It took experience and muscle—and maturity—to care for him. That kind of service was rare. She raised the phone to her ear again.

As she sat down at the table, Sarah continued talking about Acacia's needs.

When she could finally get a word in, Acacia said firmly, "Bobby's so fragile, Sarah, and with no other siblings to help, and Dad caring for Mom with her breast cancer, there's only me left. You know how old Mom and Dad are, with us being change-of-life babies. They'd never cope with what it takes to care for Bobby. And I *won't* put him in a home. I won't do that to him, Sarah. So, can we just drop this? Please?"

Before her friend could respond, Acacia changed the subject. "He has a new PT. His name's Noah."

Sarah was silent a moment. "Tell me more."

Acacia rushed on before Sarah could read anything into her bringing Noah up. "He's great with Bobby. Treats him like a child. Nobody's done that before, and it makes such a difference. I don't know why I didn't think to suggest it. Bobby really likes him. The guy brings kids' toys to work with him. It's amazing how different Bobby feels about his therapy. Noah invited us to go to the park Sunday morning, and he says he has a surprise for Bobby."

"I'm liking this already. You're getting out of the house. With a man. Oh, yes, I'm loving this," Sarah said.

Moving to the living room, Acacia picked up a couple of her brother's toys and put them in the toy box in the corner. "Would you stop that? He's Bobby's PT. This is about my brother, not me."

"What does this guy look like, anyway? Is he hot?"

Acacia's heart skipped a beat then sped up. Yes, Noah was hot. Blazing, in fact. His expressive eyes and the curly dark hair brushing the nape of his neck would fill any woman's fantasies. "Uh, he's nice-looking, I guess."

Sarah prodded her. "How nice-looking? Come on."

Acacia strode back into the kitchen and grabbed the trash bag from under the sink. This conversation had gotten way out of hand. "Okay, he's a hunk, all right? But, like I said, he's just being sweet to Bobby. He's not doing this for me."

Sarah sighed and continued. "Let's face it, hon. You're more of a mother to Bobby now than your mom is. But you're still a beautiful woman. This Noah's got eyes. He can see that."

Acacia threw open the door to the garage and dumped the bag of trash into the can. "I don't want to talk about this. He's Bobby's therapist, and that's all."

"Okay. I'm just saying, though."

"Well, don't say, okay?"

Sarah laughed. "All right, all right. You just be darn sure you have a good time on Sunday. You haven't seen the outside of your front yard unless you have a doctor's appointment or need groceries in I don't know when, so you better enjoy yourself, my friend. Or you'll answer to me."

* * *

Sunday morning, Noah checked his watch again. Acacia and her brother should have been here by now. Was there a problem? Why hadn't he offered to meet them at the house and help put Bobby in the van? How dumb could he be? He dug out his phone, but before he could call, Acacia turned into the parking lot. Waving his arm high over his head, he strode in their direction, motioning her into a parking spot near the picnic table under a tall oak tree.

As he approached them, the door slid open on Bobby's side. Noah called, "Hey there, buddy. You ready for some fun?"

Bobby swung his head toward him and moved his arms spasmodically. "Yeah." A smile lit up his face as Noah's dog, Rowdy, set his paws on the edge of the van's floor and peered inside.

Noah patted the dog's head. "This is Rowdy, my cowdog. He helps me bring the steers up when I'm roping." Motioning Rowdy up into the van, he reached for Bobby's hand. "You can pet him. Is that okay?"

A grin plastered Bobby's face. "Yeah."

Noah helped Acacia's brother stroke Rowdy's neck, and Bobby laughed when the dog licked his fingers.

Acacia got out and joined them. "Wow, he's a good-looking Border Collie. I'll bet he's a lot of help on the ranch."

A hint of her floral, spicy perfume wafted to him and he sucked in a breath. God, he loved that smell. It was different from what other women he knew wore. He could feel Acacia as if an invisible force drew them together. What was this instant attraction? It felt physical—elemental—like nothing he'd experienced before. He was in trouble. Reaching for the lock on Bobby's wheelchair, he said, "Come on. I'll help you get your brother out. You're set up over there under the tree. There are sodas for us and juice for him."

They settled in the shade, but with the temperature in the low eighties on this May morning, it was getting hot. A small tendril of hair was sweat-stuck to Acacia's temple, and Noah had to throttle the temptation to reach up and brush it away. He opened a juice packet and poured it over some ice, offering it to Bobby. "Hey, have a drink, buddy. It's hot out here." With his help, Bobby took several long swallows.

Noah set the cup on the table and clapped his hands together. "Now, are you ready for the rest of the surprise?"

Bobby's smile was his best answer.

"Okay. I've been too busy to work on Rowdy's fetching lately. I need you to lend a hand today so he doesn't forget how to do it." Noah reached into his therapy bag and pulled out a bright pink tennis ball. "Now, you knock this ball off your lap and Rowdy will run and pick it up and bring it back to you. Okay?"

"Yeah." Bobby nodded his head, still grinning.

"Rowdy? Come."

The dog trotted over and sat beside Bobby's chair.

Acacia settled at the table, out of the way.

Noah put the ball in Bobby's lap. "Now, push it off. Hard as you can."

Bobby's arms lurched into motion, nowhere near the ball.

"Slow down. You just keep trying."

In a moment, his arm flew in the ball's direction, and it rolled off his lap and down to the ground, spinning a few feet away before coming to a stop. Bobby squealed with laughter.

Acacia clapped. "That's it. You did it."

She looked different today. The sunlight made her creamy skin glow, and she seemed lighter, less worn. He wanted nothing more than to take her in his arms and brush his lips behind her ear—to make that lost look disappear from her eyes. He jerked his mind from those sensuous thoughts. The woman was Bobby's sister, for cripes' sake. He couldn't go there.

Noah motioned to Rowdy, who had been waiting patiently by the chair. "Fetch." After the dog grasped the ball in his mouth, Noah signaled to him to return it.

Raising his paws to Bobby's legs, he dropped the ball squarely into the middle of his lap.

Bobby laughed, excitement slurring his words. "Rowd-e-e-e. Rowd-e-e-e got it."

Noah squeezed Bobby's shoulder. "Yes, he did. Let's keep working with him. Knock the ball down again."

Thirty minutes later, Noah helped Bobby to empty his juice cup, as his cheeks were flushed. Heat was one of his worst enemies.

Noah touched Bobby's face and frowned. "I think it's time to get you into some air-conditioning, buddy. It got a lot warmer out here than I thought it would. Old Rowdy's had enough, too. You worked him pretty hard." Patting Bobby on the back, he looked at Acacia. "If you want to get the AC going in the van, I'll buckle him in."

"Aww," Bobby whined.

Acacia forestalled the tantrum. "How about we go home and put on *Aladdin* and have some ice cream? That'll cool us off."

All for ice cream, he went willingly to the van.

A few minutes later, Noah pulled the last tie-down strap on the wheelchair tight. "Acacia, I want to suggest something. But you have to decide what's right for your family. Have you ever thought about getting a dog?" In the close confines of the car, her perfume, slightly floral, with something a tad peppery, distracted the hell out of him. He drew in a quiet breath. She smelled so good. His body responded to her, his heart speeding and his breath quickening.

She raised her brows. "Not since we've lived here in San Antonio. No."

He tuned back in. What were they talking about? Oh, yeah. The dog. "If you're open to the idea, I'll go with you to pick one out at a shelter, and I'll help train it. It would be really good for Bobby for a number of reasons. He could be responsible for part of the dog's care, which would build his self-esteem. And he can play fetch, which I'm hoping will help him gain better control over his arms in the long term."

Acacia pressed her lips together. "I like your enthusiasm, Noah. And I appreciate everything you do for my brother. A dog's quite a responsibility, though. Let me think about it, and I'll let you know."

Noah backed out of the van and slid the door shut. As she drove out of the parking lot, he narrowed his eyes. His attraction to Acacia was getting worse. The woman drove him to distraction whenever they were together. He had to figure out what to do about it.

Chapter Two

She was sealed in the earth in a concrete coffin. Mud poured in under the lid, quickly filling the small space until it overflowed her mouth, covered her nose, and blacked out her eyes. Acacia screamed and sucked the mud deep into her lungs—and woke, gasping for breath. God, there was no going back to sleep. She threw the covers back and launched herself out of bed. This dream had been more horrific than any of its predecessors. Slick with sweat, she stripped and turned on the shower.

It didn't take rocket science to find meaning in the dream. It was all about being trapped. Imprisoned in a life with no options. Her life. She stepped into the shower. *Crap!* Adding cold to the scalding-hot water, she squeezed bath gel onto her scrubber. This was Thursday. Noah was due back. She decided to shave her legs. At least she wouldn't look like an alley cat today.

Why hadn't she heard back from the VA about that Family Caregivers Program? It had been two months since she'd sent off the paperwork. The program would make all the difference in her life. She'd use some of the money to pay a caregiver and work three twelve-hour shifts at a hospital. It was the one bright spot in her future—her real hope for change. If only someone would contact her.

Though none of her jeans fit well because of her weight loss, she picked the pair that was a little slimmer than the rest and got dressed. She even added some makeup.

The sun was peeking over the solid cedar back fence when she sat on the porch. It had been a while since she'd seen the dawn, and something about it lifted her spirits.

She sipped her hot coffee. Agreeing to marry Johnny, a rancher's son, while she was in nursing school in North Texas, had been her dream come true. Happy knowing that she'd be a rancher's wife, she'd looked forward to raising children on the ranch, and maybe going to work at a local hospital or clinic.

Bobby, her twin, the person she was closer to than anyone on earth, had wanted more from life than being a rancher, more excitement—adventure, even. He'd walked into a recruiting center one day shortly after she'd finished college and enlisted in the Army. Of course, he'd signed up to work with bomb-sniffing dogs, eventually shipping out to Kandahar. Four months into his tour, his dog had triggered an explosion, destroying the canine and nearly killing Bobby.

She and her parents had rushed to be at his side at San Antonio Military Medical Center, placing everything in their lives on hold, including her wedding.

She slammed her feet to the porch, unwilling to keep on this train of thought, and strode into the kitchen to rinse her cup.

Hours later, her traitorous heart did a flip-flop as she spied Noah through the peephole in the front door. Despite her best intentions, little tingles of excitement tickled their way up her tummy. Opening the door, she stepped back. "Come on in. We're ready today."

Why did that smile of his drive straight to her core, warming her insides like melted honey? She wouldn't allow it, damn it. She didn't need a man in her life.

Noah strode to her brother and knelt beside him. "Hey there, buddy. You want to play?" After running through a few familiar things, he introduced a new toy. "Look at this ball on a string. We're going to play baseball. I'll hold it up and you hit the ball."

From her place on the couch, Acacia shook her head. How did Noah come up with these things? The game was perfect. Her brother struggled with every muscle he could control, a huge grin on his face.

Soon, it was time to work Bobby's lower body. She moved in to help Noah put him into the lift.

Noah reached for the leg sling just as she did. Their fingers brushed. Their eyes locked. The warmth, the kindness in his eyes, wrenched at her chest.

The corner of his mouth twitched up, and he pulled the sling over and slipped it under Bobby's legs.

Her heart, which had seemed to still, beat against her ribs. This was a dangerous man. One look and she was ready to fall into his arms.

She frowned as she tightened the chest strap. Noah was bound to ask her, and she still hadn't made up her mind about whether to get Bobby a dog. No doubt it would be good for her brother, but could she add one more responsibility to her plate?

As they lowered her brother to the floor and removed the leg strap, Noah asked, "How's everything been going?"

Fragments of her nightmare flashed before her eyes. "Fine. Just fine." She could feel him watching her as she stood.

"Do you get out much? I mean, just for fun?"

What—was he fixing to ask her out? No, that was crazy. "I don't go out. I don't have anyone to stay with my brother." She sat on the couch, her hands clenched together. "My best friend is always after me to advertise for a sitter, but I haven't been able to make myself do it. Let a stranger watch him, I mean."

As he began Bobby's therapy, Noah raised his brows and waited for her to go on.

"Well, you know how fragile a quad's health is. How careful I have to be. And he's a big guy. Not just anyone can care for someone his size."

Noah neither agreed nor disagreed, so she went on. "My friend Sarah has offered to pay for the caregiver, but I'm afraid. Scared that it will be too much for whomever I hire. Scared that something might go wrong, and I won't be here."

Noah eased her brother's leg into the air, stretching muscles and tendons. "With the right person, he'll be fine. You should have time away from him. You're in this for life. Taking care of yourself is an important part of being a caregiver." He turned and his lips quirked up, his eyes filling with warmth. "I'm sure people have told you that before. It's time you started listening."

How come when Noah said it, she wanted to immediately grab her phone and place an ad? Maybe he was right, though. Help for her brother was just a matter of finding the right person. It was worth considering. After all, if she went to work, Bobby would be staying with someone else, right?

The next morning, however, she wondered what the hell she'd been thinking. Leave her brother with a sitter? She couldn't. The urine in his bag was dark yellow, a sure sign of a urinary tract infection, and though she kept the site as sterile as possible, irritation from his catheter marked a return of urethritis. His temperature was up, too. Time to call the home-based primary care service from the VA, a program available only for patients who had particularly difficult challenges getting to the VA center.

After speaking with Bobby's nurse, who would arrive later that morning to take a urine sample, Acacia emptied the bag, the ammonia smell strong in her nose, and removed his catheter. Carefully cleaning the area, she inserted a sterile catheter and put a clean diaper on him. Due to her brother's history of infections and the importance of getting on top of a bladder infection immediately, his nurse had already ordered an antibiotic. The medicine would be delivered that afternoon.

Pushing her hair back off her face, she glanced down at her brother, who lay quietly on the bed.

He grinned and swung his arm.

She patted him and leaned in, kissing his cheek. At barely nine o'clock, she was exhausted. How was she going to face a lifetime of days like this?

* * *

Tuesday morning, Noah knocked at Acacia's door, looking forward to working with her brother. And, he had to be honest, he wanted to see her too, though he knew that was wrong. But she pulled at him. Hard. He wanted to take her in his arms and make whatever haunted those beautiful brown eyes go away. He was an ass for wanting that. The woman was off-limits.

Turning his back on the door, he clenched his fists. How could he ever consider doing something more with a physical therapy business if he couldn't maintain control over his emotions? He needed to keep his eyes and his wants to himself. Acacia had her hands full, and he was here to do his best to help Bobby, not fantasize about his sister, for God's sake.

The door opened and he turned around, forcing a smile. "Hi."

"Come in. Bobby's excited to see you."

Sweeping his gaze past her, he locked on her brother, but not before noticing that she was wearing makeup. The extra color enhanced her natural beauty. Stepping through the door, he headed for his client. Had Acacia done that for him? Surely not. Maybe she was starting to feel better. He hoped so. The poor woman needed some perking up.

Bobby rocked his head back, looking up at him. "Hi."

"Hey there, buddy. How're you doing? You ready to work today?"

"Uh-huh. I wa-ant to play ball."

Noah laughed. "Okay. Batter up!" As he reached into his therapy bag for the baseball, his attention slid to where Acacia sat on the couch. She had such delicate feet for a woman so tall. Delicious, delicate, bare feet. He yanked his gaze back to his bag. Then, holding the ball on its string near Bobby's arm, he said, "Okay, buddy, let's see what you can do."

Bobby struggled to control the wild lurches of his arm, finally slugging the ball and laughing crazily.

Noah moved it a little further away as Bobby continued to swing his arm.

When Acacia left the room, Noah felt it like the passing of an electrical storm. The air of the room settled. He didn't want this to be happening—didn't want to be attracted. It was a betrayal of who he was and what he believed in. Wanting her was just plain wrong.

Sighing, he looked around him. The living room décor had kind of surprised him the first time he'd worked here. There were western prints framed in old barn wood, a sculpture made from horseshoes, and a Navajo rug on the wall. Who'd have thought? He wanted to learn more about this woman. What her background was. But that was wrong, too.

Later, as he settled Bobby back into his wheelchair, Acacia came into the room again.

"Noah, can we talk for a few minutes?"

"Sure."

"I'll fix us a glass of iced tea. We can go out on the back porch, if you don't mind. Bobby is happy watching his cartoons."

She walked in from the kitchen a couple of minutes later and led him outside.

He loved how her ponytail swung back and forth, accentuating the sexy way her hips moved. His hands should just about fit around that small waist. God help him, he'd love to wrap his hands around it right now and pull her to him. Everything about this woman drew him to her. He closed his eyes to clear the vision from his mind.

As they drank their tea, she said, "I've decided I want to get a dog. I'd like to find one already house-trained, if we can, and a large dog would be nice. I don't care for little yappers. We always had dogs on the ranch, and I enjoyed working with them. I'd like to stay away from pit bulls and pit crosses, because of the number of people I have in and out of the house. Pits seem to scare people, and I don't need that. Do you think I'm asking too much?"

"No, the shelters are full of dogs. If we don't find one we like at the first place, we'll keep looking." He took another swallow of tea. "You said 'on the ranch'. Did you live on a ranch, then?"

"I did," She grinned. "Rodeoing, the whole bit. I always thought my kids would grow up on a ranch. Life happens, though, you know?"

Drawing his brows together, he nodded. "Living in the city must be quite a change, then."

"Yep. It's taken some getting used to."

Noah set his glass on the table. "When we find a dog we like, you two can stay at the house and settle in while I go to the pet store and buy supplies. My treat. It'll be kind of hard to purchase something ahead of time until you know how large the dog is."

Frowning, she said, "You don't need to do that."

"You're right. I don't. But I want to. Listen, your brother means a lot to me." Averting his eyes, he took a swallow of tea. "He, ah...reminds me of someone."

"Really?"

Joe was someone he seldom discussed, so instead of explaining, he said, "I've gotten kind of close to a similar patient before."

Her eyes filled with sympathy. He clenched his teeth. Joe deserved her sympathy, not him. Joe was the one who'd suffered.

Speaking quickly, he said, "I like working with Bobby, making him happy. I hope you'll let me do this for him."

She nodded slowly. "Okay. For my brother, then."

* * *

That evening as Acacia relaxed on the back porch, Sarah called again. After the usual questions were asked and answered, Acacia told her, "I'm getting Bobby a dog."

"Are you sure that's wise? You already have so much going on."

"I know. I felt the same way at first. I've thought a lot about it, and it'll be good for him and might help me, too." Tucking a leg under her, she took another sip of wine.

"Really?"

"Yeah. I was thinking we'd take the dog to the park in the evenings and let him run. I'm sure Bobby would like that, and we'd be getting out of the house. I think the sunshine would really improve my mindset, too."

"I like it. You've gotten into a rut, and it's time to start doing things again. What made you consider a dog?"

Bringing up Noah would only encourage her friend to push Acacia in the man's direction again. "Ah... It was suggested as a useful part of Bobby's therapy."

"Oh. How's the hunk doing, anyway? Did you have fun at the park?"

Acacia rolled her eyes. "He brought his cowdog, Rowdy, and taught Bobby how to play fetch with him. And, yes, *my brother* had fun."

Sarah laughed. "Sensitive, aren't we?"

"He's my brother's therapist, and he's very good with him. Better than anyone who's ever worked with him, in fact. I'm not interested in Noah, though. Get that through your head, girl. I'm not looking for a man in my life. The man's not interested in me, anyway. He's all business when he's here."

Sarah was silent, so Acacia continued, "Noah said he'll come along when we pick out the dog and help train him for us."

"Well, he'll certainly spend a lot of time at your place while you train the dog. Poor you."

Acacia chuckled. "Sarah!"

"All right, all right. I'll stop."

When they hung up a few minutes later, Noah's smiling face appeared in her mind.

The man did have the best smile. Warm and kind, just like him. Sarah had brought up a good point, too. The guy would be spending time with them while he helped train their new dog. A tiny thrill rippled through her. She frowned. If this was the way she responded to the idea, how would she handle having him in such close proximity? Theirs was a professional relationship, and she must keep it that way.

* * *

Tuesday morning, Acacia handed her mom her coffee. She'd made it strong, the way her mother liked it, and the rich aroma brought back happy memories of her childhood. Their parents had come in the previous night for a visit. She enjoyed having them down for a few days each month. Their trips were the reason she'd bought a three-bedroom house. Her father doted on his wife, especially now that she was so weak from her chemo treatments for stage four breast cancer. Acacia had hoped to have a marriage like theirs when she and Johnny had gotten to-gether. The thought stabbed at her heart, hard, even after these two long years. Not so much for that asswipe Johnny anymore. He'd shown what a loser he was. She hurt for the loss of her dream.

Her mom fretted so now that she was unable to care for Acacia's dad the way she used to. He still carried on with run-ning the ranch, as well as taking on more of the cooking and cleaning while his wife lay sick in bed after her chemo treat-ments. Bobby had received his robust, blond good looks from their father. But her dad seemed paler and thinner now, and his hand had shaken when she handed him his coffee this morn-ing.

Bobby's injury had taken the stuffing out of her parents. She wished she could do more to help them. If there were any VA services for her brother near Howelton, she would have moved back there in a heartbeat.

Her parents made a six-and-a-half-hour drive each way every time they came to visit their kids. It had to be hard on her mom, as weak as she was, and they were both in their late six-ties. How much longer could they keep it up? Driving Bobby all that way was out of the question. The situation was a mess.

Acacia took a sip of her coffee. "How are things on the ranch, Dad?"

"Wheat's doing well. Calves are growing strong. We've had a little rain the past few weeks, so I'm happy. How are you? You look tired, honey."

"Oh, I'm fine. I was a little worried about Bobby. He had a UTI last week, but he's better now. You know what a trooper he is." She took another sip. "Oh, guess what? We're getting a dog." She went on to tell them all about Noah and their dog plans. "He's had Bobby playing fetch with his dog, and Bobby loved it."

Her mom raised her brows. "Your brother played fetch?"

"He sure did."

Her parents exchanged smiles.

"This Noah sounds like quite a fella," her dad said.

Acacia nodded. "The guy really has some great ideas. You'll love the things he does with Bobby."

As the women went into the kitchen to start breakfast, her mom said, "Honey, you'll never know how much it means to me and your dad that you stay with your brother. You've given up everything to do it. Most sisters would have quit by now. We wouldn't blame you if you did, sweetheart."

She reached for Acacia's hand and squeezed it gently. "We love you for caring for him, and we know it's hard for you. You're so young and talented. You could do anything with your life. Your dad and I, we hate what it's costing you. We don't know what to do to help. With this drought, the ranch isn't making much money, though your dad is working himself to the bone seven days a week. We wish we could send you more than we do."

Acacia wrapped her mom in a hug. Her blond beauty had faded some but, at sixty-eight, she could still turn heads in the older set. "You do plenty. And of course I'm here for Bobby. He's my brother." Smiling into her mom's worn face, she hoped the pep talk would work on herself too. "You and Dad need to worry about taking care of yourselves right now. I've got Bobby."

After breakfast, the doorbell rang. As she opened the door, Noah let fly with one of his heartbreaker smiles, sending an unwelcome jolt of joy through her. What had happened to her resolve to react professionally? Grimacing inwardly, she waved him in.

"Mom and Dad, this is Noah Rowden, Bobby's physical therapist. Noah, these are our parents, George and Rebecca. They're visiting for a few days from North Texas."

Noah shook hands with them both. "Nice to meet you. I sure do enjoy working with your son. He puts everything he's got into it. You raised him right."

Her parents looked at Bobby and smiled.

Acacia wondered how long it had been since they'd heard something they could be proud of about their boy. How wonderful of Noah to say that.

He knelt in front of Bobby. "You ready to get started?"

Her brother grinned. "Uh-huh."

Her mom and dad watched as Noah helped their son with his therapy, laughing at the obvious joy he got from playing "baseball."

Acacia worked at keeping her eyes on her brother and away from his therapist. It wasn't easy. Noah's tall, muscular body was like a magnet. It was hard not to notice the casual way he cocked his lean hips while he stood holding the ball on a string. She stared resolutely at Bobby as Noah's broad shoulders and long legs filled the corner of her eye. Hell, it was *impossible* to ignore him. Scrambling from the couch, she strode in to start the dishes.

As she filled the sink with hot sudsy water, she mulled over her options. Noah needed to see Bobby, that much was obvious. The problem was her. She should—what? How could she not notice a man who could easily make *People* magazine's Sexiest Man Alive? He was so damned nice, too. Good with Bobby, kind with her. She liked his holistic approach, too; he was a healer who treated the mind as well as the body. She couldn't help but think that a miracle had brought him into their lives.

Noah was perfect. And it was so unfair. Why would God put a man like this in her life when everyone knew how it would turn out? Men didn't want baggage—they wanted simple. Easy, not difficult. She knew how it worked. She'd learned the hard way. This situation was intolerable. But she had no idea what to do about it.

After therapy, Noah packed up his bag, nodding at George and Rebecca. "I'm glad I got to meet you both. I think Bobby has quite a future ahead of him. My goal is to help him gain better control of his arms. I believe your son may be able to use an electric wheelchair if we're successful." He turned to Acacia, who was sitting on the couch again. "Your daughter works with him every day, so I hope this will all make a difference."

Rebecca patted Acacia's arm. "We're so thankful for her. We know how lucky we are to have her."

Acacia pulled the door open for Noah, and he aimed a slow smile at her. Did he have to do that? Her resistance turned to mush.

"I'll see you Thursday. You take care of yourself."

Lord help her.

* * *

The next morning when Acacia offered her dad his coffee, he still appeared pale. "How are you this morning? You feeling okay?" she asked.

With a wan smile, he reached out a shaking hand. "I'm tired, I guess. Didn't sleep well. I had indigestion last night."

"I wonder if dinner caused it. Those steaks you brought were wonderful, but maybe it was a bit too heavy for you."

He scowled. "It'll be a cold day in hell, little girl, when this old rancher can't eat a good steak."

She patted his arm. "You're right. How's your stomach today?"

"Not much better, I'm afraid. I'll be fine after breakfast."

But he wasn't. She became even more concerned when she walked into the living room and saw him rubbing his chest. "Dad, is your stomach still hurting?"

"A little."

"I'm worried. You have indigestion, and you're pale. Your hand was shaking this morning, too. You could be experiencing something serious. Let's get you checked out, shall we?"

Pressing his lips together, he shook his head. "Not a chance. I'm fine. Just tired, is all. My stomach does this sometimes, too. It's no big deal." He rose from the recliner and took his coffee cup to the sink.

Her mom, who was sitting on the couch, frowned at Acacia and called after him, "George, why don't we play it safe? I'm sure you think it's nothing, but I'd feel a lot better if we checked you out."

Her dad walked back into the room and took her mother's hand. "I'll be fine, honey. Don't you worry about me. Emergency rooms cost too much, and there's no need to spend that kind of money right now on an upset stomach."

Acacia knew a losing battle when faced with one. "Dad, will you at least see the doctor when you get home?"

"Sure, sure. I will."

Well, that was the best she could do. She only hoped it would be enough.

* * *

The following Saturday, Noah's gaze followed Acacia as she struggled to push Bobby up the ramp near the front door of the animal shelter. Everything about caring for her brother was hard. He was a big man, and though she wasn't a small woman, she was thin—worn down, in his opinion. Teaching her brother to use an electric wheelchair would help Acacia in so many ways. Bobby would always be childlike, needing adult supervision, but being able to direct his own powered wheelchair would literally take a heavy burden from his sister.

God, he admired her. How many women would do what she was doing? Care for a brother who didn't remember her? Who had a childlike mind? Who was dependent on her for every physical and emotional need? Not many. And it cost her. Terribly, if appearances were to be believed.

He was having a hard time keeping his emotions detached when he was around her, no matter how many times he told himself that he needed to. All he wanted to do was take her frail-seeming body into his arms and give her his strength. Tell her that she wasn't alone in her struggle. To provide a sanctuary, even for a short time, where she didn't bear all the burden.

Slamming the door on the van, he followed the two inside the building.

The sound of barking dogs and the smell of wet disinfectant hit him as he entered the shelter. They had probably just cleaned the cages.

Acacia stood at the front desk with her brother. "We're looking for a larger breed, preferably housebroken. We don't mind an older dog. Not too awfully old, though, as we want him or her around for a few years. Do you have anything like that here? This is the second place we've visited today."

The young woman at the counter, who said her name was Ellie, smiled. "I think we have some that might work. Why don't you all follow me to the back?"

Noah walked behind them, trying to keep his eyes off Acacia's slim body and on the dogs in the kennels. But it wasn't working. He wondered whether she was the kind of girl whose knees got weak when she was aroused. If he kissed her, would she wrap her arms around his neck and hold on tight? He shook his head to clear the image. This was crazy.

About halfway down the aisle, they stopped in front of a cage holding a mid-sized dog that appeared to be a mixture of—a shepherd and some kind of terrier? Wow.

Ellie opened the cage and bent to pet the dog. "This is a female named Bonnie. She's house-trained, and she's six years old."

Acacia turned to Noah. "She's a bit small, isn't she?"

"You pick what you feel comfortable with."

She asked, "Have you heard her bark? Is it high-pitched?"

Ellie grinned. "Yeah. I'll be honest. She leans more toward the little dog in her bark."

Acacia pressed her lips together. "Let's see what else you have."

The next one Ellie led them to was bigger, but had long, curly hair. Opening the cage, she knelt, giving the dog a hug. "This is Charlie. He's housebroken. His owners moved to an apartment that doesn't allow pets. He's five."

Acacia frowned. "He looks sweet, but that coat of his must take lots of work. Is he part sheepdog?"

Ellie shrugged. "I don't know. He'll take some extra care, but he's really a sweetie. I hope he'll go to a happy home."

"I'm sure he is, but I'm worried I won't have the time to care for hair like that. Can you show me what else you have?"

Ellie shut the gate and headed off down the aisle, talking over her shoulder. "This last one is a bit lazy, but he's a sweetheart, too."

On the farthest aisle over, she stopped in front of a cage holding a behemoth.

Noah's eyes widened. What exactly was this animal? He looked like he had some Great Dane in him, and probably mastiff, too. He was so muscled up, though. What else did he have in him? The dog lay on the floor, only raising his eyebrows when they approached.

Ellie opened the cage and leaned down to pet him. Lifting his head, he licked her hand, then returned his head to his paws. "This is Bobo. The family's baby named him. They're military, and the dad got orders for an overseas deployment, so the dog ended up with us. Since we're a no-kill shelter, they hoped he'd find a good home. Bobo is great with kids and has never met a stranger he doesn't like. He knows how to walk on a lead, and he's housebroken."

Acacia entered the cage and knelt. "Hey, Bobo, would you like to come home with us? We have a backyard for you to play in." She stroked her hand down his back. "Ellie, how long has he been here?"

"We just got him. I'm sure we'll place him fast. Being housebroken and such a good-looking dog, he won't have a hard time finding a home."

"How old is he?"

"He's three."

Acacia patted his head and stood. "Bobo doesn't look like much of a barker. Is that true?"

Ellie laughed. "Barking takes effort. Bobo's more on the reserved side, as you can see."

"Can you lead him out?"

Ellie led him from the cage, and Acacia said, "Bobby, this guy's name is Bobo. Would you like him to come live with us?"

Bobby laughed, his arms moving erratically. "Yeah, Bobo can sleep with me."

Acacia smiled and looked at Noah. "I think we've found us a dog."

He pressed his lips together. God, she was beautiful when she was happy. Bobo looked like the perfect dog for her brother. His head was above the arm of Bobby's chair—easy for him to connect with for petting—or what would pass for it, with Bobby's aim. Bobo could easily drop the tennis ball in his lap.

Acacia had made a great choice. Now it was a matter of training the dog. Noah sighed. Would he be able to stay professional spending so much time around Bobby's beautiful sister?

While Acacia loaded her brother into the van, Noah took Bobo out to his truck. The dog rode calmly in the back seat on the return trip to the house. Using a piece of rope, he led Bobo up the ramp and inside the front door. Bobby waited excitedly in the living room. The dog, as if knowing who his new master was to be, walked straight to the wheelchair and flopped down at Bobby's feet.

Acacia turned from watching Bobo, her eyes glistening with unshed tears. "I'm so glad you encouraged me to get a dog. He's perfect."

Noah shoved his hands in his back pockets. She was gorgeous. And brave. And so untouchable. Kneeling in front of Bobby, he ruffled Bobo's ears.

The dog raised his eyebrows and huffed out a warm breath.

With a last pat, Noah stood and headed to the door. "Will Bobo sleep inside or outside at night?"

"He's housebroken, so in the house, I guess."

"Okay. I'll be back in an hour or so with his stuff."

* * *

Noah waited for Acacia to answer the door. He'd had an idea while shopping for Bobo's things and couldn't wait to share it with her.

She opened the door and as he stepped inside, he said, "I think I'm going to change my therapy time to late afternoon, if you don't mind. That way I can spend more time with Bobo and Bobby."

She shrugged. "Afternoons are fine with me."

After sitting on the couch, he laid everything he'd brought in front of him.

She knelt on the floor and helped him unpack.

He'd bought a memory foam bed pad that fit the gargantuan canine still lying at Bobby's feet, and a tall feeding stand with food and water bowls built in. This was a must with a dog whose head was so high off the ground. Of course, he'd purchased an extra-large choke collar and a leather leash. With Bobo's personality, he didn't see Acacia needing the choke chain, but with such a large dog, having control was important if she needed it. After he'd found healthy food for a dog Bobo's size, the final purchase had been a cylinder of tennis balls.

He opened the tube and held one up in front of Bobby. "I bought balls so we can teach Bobo how to fetch."

Bobby threw his head back and laughed. "Bobo can fetch."

He put the ball back in the tube. "That's right. Bobo lives here now, and you and I will work with him. It'll be lots of fun."

As Noah stood to leave, Acacia got up and took his hand in both of hers.

"How can I ever thank you? You've made such a difference in our lives. You've given us something to look forward to, I guess." She spoke softly. "Just, thank you."

His heart leapt. Her soft, smooth palm on the back of his hand stirred him. He wanted to lean into her gaze until his lips touched hers, but he couldn't. Instead, he replied, "You're so welcome. I enjoy the time I spend with you all."

He shut the front door and walked down the ramp, overcome with forbidden *if only*s.

Chapter Three

Tuesday morning, Acacia opened the door for Noah, bracing herself for the sight of the man's way-too-hot body. The first thing he did was hand her a piece of paper. Reading the note, she asked, "What's this?"

As he came in the door, he said, "The name of someone who's willing to learn to care for Bobby. Jenny's a college student who grew up with my sister. I've known her for ages. She's strong, and she's dependable." Placing his hands on his hips, he said, "I talked to her Sunday. She's been looking for a way to earn extra money. She can help you out around her class schedule. I hope you'll call her. It's a perfect solution for both of you."

Sitting on the couch, she reread the note. "Well, I mean, of course I'll call her." Reading it again, she chewed the inside of her cheek. "Yeah, this is a good thing. Thanks."

"You bet."

Acacia folded and unfolded the paper. This was happening. What she'd hoped for. Could she go through with it, though? What if something happened to Bobby? Jenny was just a college student. How well could she do the job? *Dammit. Stop it! You always talk yourself out of finding help. It's time to do it.* Walking into the kitchen, she trapped the note under a butterfly magnet on the refrigerator door. She'd call today. No backing out this time.

As Noah worked with Bobby, her mind roamed over the ways her life had changed since he'd come into it. And he was so kind and encouraging with her brother. Then there were his knockout looks. He appeared to be the perfect man, yet she knew from experience that appearances could be deceiving. Despite how her body reacted to him, she'd be stupid to let down her guard.

Before Noah left for the day, he took her hand in his calloused one and covered it with his other. "Acacia, I know how hard it is for you to allow someone else to take care of Bobby, but this is important. You need to be around for him for many years to come. Please call Jenny. She's a competent young woman."

Warmth flooded through her, racing from the hand he held to her heart. The sense of being enveloped by Noah filled her, and she wanted more. "Yes, I'll call. Thank you so much for recommending her."

What would it feel like to have his strong arms encircle her, to snuggle her cheek against the muscles of his chest? Would he kiss her gently, or would he hunger for her lips, possessing every inch of her mouth until she had no breath left in her lungs? She blinked, frowning.

He squeezed her hand a final time and walked out the door.

She stood alone, bereft of his touch.

* * *

Thursday afternoon, Acacia sat in the shade on her back porch, watching Noah work with Bobby and Bobo under the oak tree. The man had such patience. The poor dog; each time he fetched the ball, he dropped it in Bobby's lap and flopped down on the grass, as if hoping his part were over for the day. His shelter caretaker had been right. Bobo was a lazy boy.

Under Noah's tutelage, however, he'd learned to fetch quickly. As soon as Bobby sent the ball spinning away from his chair, Bobo was up and after it without being told. He really was the perfect dog for her brother. His head was at a height where Bobby's arm could connect with it in a crazy kind of caress. Though it was seldom a gentle touch, Bobo recognized it as his master's way of petting him and responded with a lick of his soft tongue.

The fetch game finished up, and she walked over and squatted next to Bobo, wrapping her arms around his large muscular neck. "You're a smarty-pants, do you know that? And you're a good boy." Rubbing his jowls, she kissed him on the nose, crooning, "I love you, oh, yes I do." She smiled up at Noah. "I can't believe we lucked out with this guy. Isn't he perfect?"

Noah knelt beside her and patted the dog's broad haunches. "He's something, all right."

Noah was so close. The hairs on her arm stood up as if an electrical charge passed through them. The warmth emanating from Noah's strong, hard body lit up her senses, and she sucked in a breath. Biting at the corner of her mouth, she asked herself why they couldn't just be friends. She needed one here in San Antonio in the worst possible way, and who said that her friends always had to be women? Noah possessed every trait she looked for—honesty, loyalty, kindness, a sense of humor. Why shouldn't it work?

Before she could change her mind, she stood and dusted off her hands. "Noah, I want to thank you, as a friend, for everything you've done for Bobby. Will you come to dinner sometime?"

He rose to his feet and smiled. "I'd like that."

A thrill rushed through her. He'd said yes! "Are weeknights or weekends better for you?"

Pursing his lips, he said, "Well, anytime, really, except I'm usually practice-roping on Friday nights and at a roping on Saturdays. Other than that, I'm always around."

"How about this Sunday, then, say about five o'clock?" She bit her bottom lip.

"That sounds great."

Whew! Okay, now what should she fix for dinner? "What's your alcoholic beverage of choice?"

"Miller Lite."

"We're all set, then. I'm so glad you can come. Bobby'll be excited." She had to admit it, so was she.

After he left, she settled her brother in front of the TV and started supper. This was a Hamburger Helper night, so she dumped a package of thawed hamburger in a skillet and turned on the heat. Having Noah here for a longer period in the afternoons was perfect. He seemed determined to help Bobby hone his skills with his forearms.

Running water into a small pot, she dropped some tea bags into it and set it on the stove to heat. She admitted it: therapy had become her favorite part of the day. The listless feeling that had haunted her for months had disappeared. No longer was she just going through the motions with Bobby's therapy. His hard work had a goal now. Everything was so different with Noah in the picture. In her mind, she called him her miracle cowboy now.

After stirring the meat, she poured herself a glass of wine and walked into the living room to check on Bobby.

Tired from his therapy, he leaned his head back against his chair, engrossed in his cartoons.

A light had come on inside her brother when Noah entered his life. Laughter and anticipation for his day was part of his new norm. She hadn't realized what had been missing until she experienced her brother's newfound joy. She'd wasted two long years being scared and feeling sad for him and sorry for herself. That time was over. From now on, she would make sure her brother had plenty of reasons to be happy.

When supper was ready, she moved a chair and wheeled her brother to the kitchen table. "Let's eat up, big guy. Then you can pick out your stories. How about we read three books tonight?" A spoonful at a time, she fed him his dinner, while carrying on a conversation about Bobo, Noah, and their mom and dad. She talked about their parents often to Bobby. Though he didn't remember his past, she wanted him to love his parents now. He needed that security.

After she read Bobby his stories and settled him into bed for the evening, she took her wine to the darkened back porch. This being Texas, she turned the light on and checked for snakes before stepping out. Sitting back in her comfortable chair, she looked into the sky, missing the star-filled nights on the North Texas ranch where she'd grown up. Here in San Antonio, the city lights overwhelmed the glow of the stars.

A familiar heaviness sat on her chest. She missed her family. She missed her friends. She missed... She missed feeling loved, being held in a man's arms. She missed everything she'd thought her life would become before Bobby returned from Afghanistan. But she didn't miss the man who'd promised to marry her. The man she'd loved who'd broken her heart. This missing was nameless—a strong, hard yearning without a face. If she wasn't careful, though, this yearning would soon have a name—Noah.

Swallowing a large gulp of wine, she wiped her lips. Shameless. That was what she was. Obviously any man would do. She hardly knew Noah, and look at her. She *needed* him. She *wanted* him. She was selfish! Her brother had lost everything. He couldn't even *want* anymore. Didn't understand it. He was owed. He earned being cared for the day that bomb took his whole life from him. And by God, she wouldn't be the woman who let him down.

* * *

Noah knocked at the door at five sharp Sunday afternoon, passing the bouquet of flowers from hand to hand, still unsure if they were too much. He'd finally bought them, deciding that a friend could bring flowers. Then he'd second-guessed himself all the way to Acacia's house. He didn't want her to think he was being forward. Hell, he just hoped they were all right.

Acacia opened the door, and his eyes widened. Long dark curls massed around her shoulders. It was clear she'd spent a lot of time on her appearance. Her bright sundress showed off her clear complexion and her red lipstick. She looked like a model—a gorgeous one. How was he supposed to be detached, only a friend, with her looking like this? His body was already on alert and he'd just arrived.

She smiled and clasped her hands behind her back before moving away from the door. "What beautiful flowers. Thank you, Noah. Come in." Taking the bouquet from him, she said,

"I'm just finishing up dinner. Nothing fancy, spaghetti and garlic bread. Salad. Would you like a beer?"

"Sure. That'd be nice."

She hesitated, then rushed to say, "I'll just put these in water. Be right back."

Bobby was in the living room and cried out, "Noah," as he entered.

He walked over and gave Bobby a hug. "How're you doing, buddy?"

Bobby moved his arms erratically, trying to hug him back. "Good."

Bobo lay next to his master's wheelchair, eyes closed and oblivious to his surroundings.

Acacia came in from the kitchen and handed Noah a beer. "I'm toasting the bread. It'll be a couple more minutes."

The warmth from her smile washed through him. He didn't know how to react to this rocking-hot Acacia. He knew what he *wanted* to do. He wanted to pull her into his arms and kiss her red lips, to run his fingers through her long curls, to cup her face and look deep into those dark, easy-to-read eyes. Would he find a desire in them to match his own? God, he had a whole evening of this temptation to get through. "I can't wait for dinner. I came hungry."

"Great, because I made plenty. Do you want to bring Bobby in while I set out the food?"

As he wheeled her brother to the kitchen, he willed his pulse to slow and tamped down on his anticipation. She'd said *friend*, right? Lord, he wanted more from this woman. Every inch of her beckoned to him. When he was near her, friendship was the last thing on his mind.

She pulled a chair away from the table to make room for her brother's wheelchair as she headed to the stove. Taking the garlic bread out from under the broiler, she popped the slices into a basket and covered it with a hand towel to keep it warm. After placing the basket and the tea pitcher on the table, she went back for the bowls of spaghetti and salad, then joined Noah and Bobby.

"I don't make very traditional spaghetti. No meatballs. I brown my hamburger meat, mix it in my sauce, and when it's finished simmering, I pour the whole lot on my noodles and stir it all together. My mom always made it that way, so I do, too."

Noah took a long, deep sniff. "It looks and smells delicious. Who cares how traditional it is?"

Acacia grinned. "I'll say grace and we can dig in."

She extended her hand, and his heart skipped a beat in anticipation of her touch. Clasping her fingers, he reached over for Bobby's hand.

Bowing her head, she prayed, "God, thank You for all our blessings and for this food we're about to eat. Thank You for our family and friends. We love You and pray this in Your Son, Jesus's name, amen."

Noah raised his head and let go of her hand, feeling the loss of her touch immediately. It was wonderful to be here with Acacia dishing up the plates and the three of them sitting like a family around the dinner table. What would it be like to come home to this every night? A vision of her moving comfortably around his kitchen at the ranch came to him, and his heart gave a quick triple-beat. Yes, wouldn't that be awesome? But that dream was impossible when Bobby was his client. Reaching for the plateful of spaghetti Acacia handed him, he smiled his thanks.

She passed the bread basket. "Try this. My mom makes her garlic bread this way. I love it."

Taking the basket, he pulled out a couple of slices. "Sounds like your mom is a good cook." He tried the spaghetti. "This tastes wonderful."

"Thanks. Actually, my mom is a great cook, and she taught me everything I know. Mom helped my dad out on the ranch when we were growing up, so she showed me how to do a lot of the cooking and cleaning." She gave Bobby a bite of spaghetti and continued, "Mom and I planted and tended our vegetable garden. I miss it, living here in the city, so I have a container garden on my back porch. It fills my need to grow things." After tasting her own spaghetti, she gave Bobby another bite.

Noah drew his brows together. "You've been a kind of caregiver all your life. No wonder you're so good with Bobby."

"Well, I went to college. Earned my bachelor's degree. I'm an RN."

Noah smiled and took another bite of spaghetti. "So, you're a *highly trained* caregiver. Bobby is a lucky guy, indeed."

She tilted her head toward him. "What was your childhood like, Noah?"

He studied his plate. His early years were so bound up with mixed emotions about Joe that his childhood was something he rarely talked about. When he met her gaze, he said, "My dad and I worked on the ranch, of course. And Dad taught me to rope. He took me around to ropings, supported me competing. At first I calf roped, then I started team roping. I rodeoed in college and got my degree in physical therapy. Then I went ahead and got my Master's. Eventually, I want to open my own PT business."

"Noah, it's a wonderful plan. Just think how many lives you can impact that way. How soon do you think you'll do it?"

"I've been putting money aside for quite a while now, and I have a business plan. It won't be too long." Her encouragement warmed him more than he'd expected. More than even the support of his parents. Somehow, in the short time he'd known her, her opinion had come to matter tremendously. He sucked in his lower lip. When, exactly, had that happened?

After dinner, they all went out to the backyard and sat in the shade of the tall oak tree while Bobby and Bobo played some fetch. Noah marveled at the way Bobby was now able to play the game without help. Each time, Bobo placed the ball in the center of Bobby's lap, and Bobby swung much more accurately at it, knocking the ball to the ground after only a try or two. The game was still a work in progress, but Noah could see that great headway was being made.

Acacia reached over and laid her hand on Noah's arm. "Bobby is having so much fun, and it's all thanks to you. He's happy now. I don't know how to thank you."

His pulse sped up at her gentle touch. It made him need more. "My reward is Bobby's progress. When one of my clients shows improvement, even a small amount like Bobby's, it's like my life has a purpose. Like I'm doing what I've always wanted."

She gazed down at her lap. "Six months ago, I never dreamed I could be so full of hope."

She turned to him, and her sweet smile stunned him with shivers of desire. He spread his hands across his tense thighs, pressing hard, yet his body responded to her pleasure despite his effort at restraint. "If you don't mind, I'll round up another beer." He headed quickly toward the house.

Inside, he pressed the cold beer to his forehead. He wanted her, dammit. Not as a friend, as something more. How long had it been since he'd felt this way about a woman? He'd been attracted to women, of course. But this—this gut-level need—was different. The thing he had for Acacia was consuming him at the oddest times. When he was roping, filling out paperwork, or feeding the stock, he found her in his head. He had to do something about it. She'd said he was her friend, but friendly wasn't how he felt about her.

Looking down, he checked himself out. It was safe to go back outside, but he still had no answer to his problem.

* * *

Late Friday afternoon, Acacia glanced over as her phone navigation said, "You have reached your destination." Though Noah had given her directions, it had been comforting to have her GPS as backup while she drove into the Texas Hill Country toward his ranch. Stopping at the big metal gate, she reached out her window to the keypad and entered the code he'd given her. The lock clicked as it disengaged, and the gate swung open.

Glancing in the rearview mirror at her brother, she said, "We're here. It's just a little farther to the barn."

Noah had asked her Tuesday if she and Bobby would like to come to roping practice at his arena. She couldn't remember the last time she'd gone on an actual outing with Bobby and had readily agreed.

The barn and arena came into view, and a few seconds later, there was Noah. The harsh, afternoon sunlight and shadows loved the sharp planes and rounded muscles of his masculine body—one God had made to sexy perfection.

He raised his arm and waved, heading in their direction.

As she pulled next to the arena, Noah walked up to her window and took off his hat. "Hi." Leaning in a little, he looked back at Bobby. "Hey there, partner, you ready to see some roping?"

His amazing smell sent her pulse pounding. She wanted to run her fingers through his hair, which was just inches from her face. That woman-killer smile, though aimed at Bobby, still slayed her. She gulped and turned her head away, holding her breath.

"Yeah! I want to," Bobby yelled.

Noah patted Acacia's shoulder.

At his touch, a rush of excitement zipped through her belly. Her pulse roared in her ears like a jet engine, and his smell still filled her nose. She never should have accepted this invitation.

He pushed away from the truck and returned his hat to his head. "Follow me, and I'll show you where I have you all set up."

Driving behind him, she was keenly aware of the sexy swivel of his hips and every swing of his broad, muscular shoulders. Drawing in a deep breath, she exhaled slowly.

Noah motioned for her to stop under several tall oak trees, where she saw a comfortable-looking lawn chair and an ice chest. There was also a large circular fan for Bobby so that he wouldn't overheat. Extension cords ran all the way from the barn. The man had thought of everything.

After he helped them get settled, Noah said, "I need to go warm up. We'll get started roping in a few minutes. When we stop to let the horses blow, I'll bring Red, that's my horse, over so Bobby can meet him."

He squeezed her shoulder as he turned and walked toward the arena gate.

The impression of his fingers lingered. Each time he touched her, she ached for more. *Friendship, Acacia*, she kept having to remind herself. *Friendship*.

There were four cowboys practicing tonight: Noah and his partner, Ronnie, and another team that they regularly traveled to ropings with. A teenager was running the head gate of the chute, and his job was to release the steers for the ropers.

The cowboys cantered around the arena, shaking out their loops and swinging them over their heads, getting the kinks out. Acacia's gaze stayed glued to Noah as his body swung easily with Red's rhythmical movement, the beat of the horse's hooves lulling her senses. Her concentration snapped as Ronnie rode up and blocked Noah from her view. *Come on, Acacia. Get a grip*. She turned to Bobby. "Hey, how about some juice?"

Keeping her back to the arena, she opened a juice pack and jammed the straw in the hole. After giving Bobby several sips and adjusting the angle of the fan, she walked over to the van and fiddled around inside, cleaning up a few scraps of trash. When she couldn't put it off any longer, she picked up the photos she'd brought with her and headed back to her chair.

Leaning close to Bobby, she held a picture in front of him. "Did you know that you and I used to ride horses together? This is us when we were kids." Being twins, they'd done everything together, and that meant that they'd both had horses. She pointed to a boy of about seven with a head full of blond curls sitting on a tall and obviously older horse. "This is you, Bobby."

Her brother threw back his head and laughed. "I can ride a horse."

She couldn't help but giggle at his response. His arm reached awkwardly for the photo. She put it in his hand and helped him hold onto it. Moving it closer to his face, she said, "Look how well you rode. We each had our own horse back then, and after school and on the weekends we rode all over the ranch."

Bobby couldn't hold his arm still for long, even with her help, and the photo soon ended up on his lap. She held up another one of him loping past the camera.

Bobby laughed again. "I go fast, 'Cacia!"

She patted his back. "You sure did. You were a good rider, brother. We used to give our horses baths down at the barn."

Bobby drew his eyebrows together.

She laughed when she realized what he must have been imagining. "Not in a bathtub, silly. We got them wet with the water hose and scrubbed them with a big sponge."

Bobby's face cleared and he grinned. "I like the water hose, 'Cacia."

She chuckled, remembering the times in the past two years that she'd taken him into the backyard and played in the water with him. He couldn't feel the liquid on his body, but he loved it on his face. He'd cracked up when she'd tucked the hose with a sprayer on the end under his arm and then screamed when he'd squirted water on her.

She glanced at the arena. It looked like the guys were ready to rope. The steers milled around in the holding pen, and one stood fretting in the chute. A breeze gusted from that direction, and she smelled fresh manure from the anxious cattle. Two cowboys on their mounts backed into the roping boxes on either side of the chute, their ropes raised at shoulder height. The header nodded, and—like a shot—the chute flew open. The steer broke out, and the horses lurched into motion. The header galloped close behind the steer and let his loop fly, catching both horns. He yanked his slack and wrapped his dally around the horn, turning his horse and jerking the steer sideways. This threw the steer off his stride, his heels flying in the air. The second cowboy threw his loop and captured both heels, whipping his slack back and dallying around the horn while turning his horse to face his partner, who had done the same. They backed up, stretching the steer tightly between them.

Acacia clapped and yelled, "Woohoo. Way to go." They'd made good time. Seven seconds.

The cowboys nodded and grinned as they released the steer from their ropes.

Now Noah and Ronnie had their horses in the boxes. The steer was in the chute, with the boy poised at the head gate. Red pranced his front feet, his weight back on his haunches as he stared at the steer, ready to go. Noah nodded, and *bam!* the gate shot open and the steer bolted free. Noah and Red were on him in two leaps of the horse's long legs. Noah's loop caught both horns, and he swung Red hard to the left. Ronnie captured the heels, and both cowboys turned, stretching the steer between them.

Acacia checked her watch. Not quite five seconds. It might even have been better if she'd had a stopwatch. Jumping to her feet, she yelled, "Yes! All right! Great time, guys!"

Noah doffed his hat and waved, grinning.

She grinned back. That face could light the Milky Way. The man was downright gorgeous when he smiled like that.

Sitting back down, she was amazed at how good the two were. Their time would stand in the pro circuit. Seriously.

Bobby, who had yelled along with her, had a happy smile on his face. She was so glad she'd said yes to Noah's invitation. She'd worried about the heat, but in true Noah fashion, he'd taken care of that. The fan kept Bobby cool under the shade of the trees. How had she been so lucky? She'd never imagined that Bobby could still find joy in his life, and yet look at him sitting there, smiling from ear to ear, taking in everything around him. This was all Noah's doing.

Rising, she stepped over to give Bobby some more juice and a few chips. After his third bite, she said, "This is fun, isn't it?"

"Uh-huh. I like cows. Ho-orses go fast."

She helped him with a last sip of juice. "Yes, they do, don't they? I'm having fun, too." A horse snorted and stamped its foot nearby, and she turned toward the arena. Noah and Red stood near the fence. His face held her transfixed. On it was the intense look of a man who wanted, and wanted bad. Then it was gone.

He nodded. "You all doing okay?"

Shaken, she answered, "Ah, sure. We're great. Thanks for the drinks and snacks. You really went to a lot of trouble." What did that look mean? Was he attracted to her? Did he dream of her the way she fantasized about him?

Touching the brim of his hat, he said, "I'm glad you all came." The head gate clanged open, and he turned Red toward the action in the arena.

Settling back into her chair, she crossed her legs, picking at the seam of her Wranglers. That look... How in the world could Noah be interested in her when her life was such a mess? Who in their right mind would be drawn to what she had to offer? Johnny had sure turned tail and run. But Noah Rowden was a good man. And he cared for her brother.

Later, while the others tied their horses to the fence to rest, Noah led his horse over to them. He squatted down in front of Bobby, holding the reins loosely in his hands. "Hey, buddy, this here's Red. Would you like to pet him?"

Bobby tilted his head to the side and grinned. "Yeah."

Noah pulled Red close, right beside Bobby, and helped him reach out and touch Red on his shoulder. He rubbed her brother's hand in the sweat near the cinch and held it to Bobby's nose. "This is what horses smell like. What do you think?"

Bobby sniffed. "I like horses."

The horse turned his head and eyed them.

Bobby laughed. "Hi, Red."

Acacia smiled at her brother's words.

"Horses have different feet than we do. Here, let me show you." Noah eased Red out a bit and lifted his leg. "See, his foot is round, and this outside is hard." Noah pulled a metal hoof pick out of his back pocket and tapped on the outer hoof, making a clacking sound. "Hear that? Now listen to this." He tapped on the inside of the hoof. "See, this is soft, so it sounds different. It even sounds kind of hollow, like a drum." Letting go of the hoof, he said, "Red's big, isn't he?"

Bobby's eyes grew wide. "Yeah, he's big, Noah."

"But there are little horses called Shetland ponies and even littler horses called minis. They're as small as your wheelchair."

"I want a little horse, Noah."

Noah grinned. "I think that sounds like fun, too." He walked Red over and tied him to the arena fence. When he came back, he opened up another chair that had been leaning against a tree, popped open a can of beer from the ice chest, and sat next to Acacia.

After taking a long swallow, he turned to her, a hint of that previous intense emotion in his gaze.

It sparked an answering need in her. Her lips parted, and she couldn't tear her gaze from his. His eyes dipped deep into her soul, where her secrets lay. Did he see how she felt about him—how she wanted him? Twisting her head away, she said, "Bobby, are you thirsty?" and got up to give him a drink.

When she was back in her chair again, Noah asked, "Have you been able to contact Jenny yet?"

More than ready to move to this safe subject, she said, "Oh, yeah. We're getting together Sunday. She sounds wonderful, Noah. I called my friend Sarah and told her about Jenny, and she said to tell you thanks."

"I hope it all works out. Keep me posted, will you?"

"Sure." Rowdy had been around all afternoon, and when he ran over again, she stroked his head.

At the next break, Noah walked back over and sat down next to her.

Acacia handed him a cold beer. "We need to get home pretty quick. Bobby's used to hitting the sack about now. I don't want him to get tired and cranky after such a happy day."

"I wouldn't want that either, but I hate to see you go."

A little while later, Noah gave Bobby a goodbye hug and helped Acacia load him into the van. He shut the sliding door and asked, "Do you remember how to get back out to the highway?"

"I think so. If not, there's always GPS."

He reached for her hand and squeezed her fingers gently. "I'm so glad you came."

Without thinking, she pulled him into a hug. His smell, a little sweaty mixed with the cologne she loved, sang to her senses. As he wrapped his arms around her, she closed her eyes. Warmth swirled into her from Noah's body pressed so close to hers. How she'd missed the sense of security from a man's arms squeezing her tight. It was impossible to pull away. Resting her cheek on his shoulder, she whispered, "I'm glad I came, too." After leaning her forehead against him for a moment, she sighed and stepped back.

Placing a fingertip under her chin, he tilted her gaze to his. "I'll see you Tuesday."

God, that look. The man *did* want her. Eyes wide, trembling, she swung her door open and climbed inside. Starting the engine, she glanced back at him, hoping he couldn't read her emotions. "Goodbye, Noah. See you then."

Chapter Four

Noah's heart galloped toward the finish line as the van turned past the barn and headed down the drive to the gate. The memory of Acacia's warm body pressed against him tweaked his every sense. He smelled the subtle sweet perfume of her hair, felt the soft rise of her breasts against his chest, and relived her fingers sliding up the muscles of his back as they rose to his shoulder blades. He'd wanted to kiss her so badly. It had taken every ounce of his self-control to hold back, to merely return her hug in the most platonic way.

It had been great having her here tonight, but he'd had a terrible time concentrating, surprising himself each time he'd caught both horns on his steer. He could feel her watching. Even when he wasn't looking, his attention had been on the woman and her brother sitting under the trees.

Her beauty wasn't what attracted him most. Pretty women were easy to come by. It was her goodness, her devotion, her—what? Her moral code? Was that what made her catch and keep his undivided attention? He needed to know all about her. What did she think of? What did she dream of? What made Acacia Richards tick?

Heading back to the arena, he was sure of something. She was worth finding out those answers.

* * *

Acacia lit a candle on the small table beside her porch chair and picked up her glass of wine. Bobby was in bed, and she craved the silence. Curling her leg underneath her, she peered into the night sky, where the bright lights from the airport to the northeast caused an unnatural glow.

She was both exhilarated and confused since she'd hugged Noah Friday night. Tomorrow was Tuesday, and she'd see him. How the hell should she act? On the surface, their hug had been simple. In reality, it had rocked her world.

Gulping some more wine, she wiped the back of her hand across her mouth. She was being stupid, but she couldn't make herself stop wanting him. He terrified her, and yet he was irresistible.

She brought her legs up and wrapped her arms around them. With her chin resting on her kneecaps, she tried to make sense of her feelings. There was no avoiding the fact that she wanted the man. The feeling was real and honest. But how did she know that he wouldn't turn tail and run like Johnny had from the responsibility that Bobby represented in her life? She couldn't know. That was the problem.

Her situation was impossible, dammit. She wanted and she ached and she desperately needed to fall asleep against a man's chest every night. The thing was, her twin, her only sibling, slept alone and helpless in a room inside her house. And she was the only one who could care for him. And all this, her needs and her wants, were denied because she alone could care for her brother.

Slow, hot tears filled her eyes, and she bit her lip hard. Then harder. Tears spilled down her cheeks, splashed onto her knees. She had no hope. There was no answer to the trap life had made for her. If she remained honorable, true to her beliefs, this was how her life would be.

She closed her eyes, and Noah's arms slid around her, holding her close. His chin rested lightly against her hair. How could she bear to lose that? She sucked in a breath and whimpered. *Oh, Christ in heaven, help me. I'm lost. I don't know how to live like this forever.*

She reached for her phone and dialed Sarah. Her friend answered, but Acacia couldn't speak. Instead, she broke into sobs.

"What is it, honey? What's wrong?" Sarah begged her.

She cried, "I don't know. I can't think." Such misery, such hopelessness, swallowed her. She couldn't bear to live the lonely life that stretched ahead of her to eternity.

After a while, her sobbing slowed. Sniffing hard, she wiped her nose on the back of her hand. "I'm sorry. I shouldn't have called while I was this upset."

"No, honey. I'm glad you did. Just tell me."

Acacia sucked in a breath and sobbed once, then bit her lip and held it, waiting it out. "I think I've hit a wall."

"Tell me. Did something bring this on? What happened?"

Bit by bit, she told Sarah how, while working for Bobby, Noah had made his way into her heart. About going to his ranch Friday, and the hug they'd shared. "I'm terrified. Look at my life. Look what happened with Johnny. And I'm not protecting myself. I'm too needy."

"Acacia, there's nothing wrong with you. And life has more good things in store for you. I *think* I know what I'd do in your place, but in reality, nobody knows until they've walked in your shoes. All I can tell you, honey, is that you're a strong person who deserves love. You remember that as you work your way through this."

Acacia sighed heavily and looked out into the city's starless sky. "Thanks. I'll keep trying. I promise. What would I do without you?"

Sarah blew her a kiss. "You won't ever have to find out. I hope you can sleep tonight. Have faith. God loves you, and so do I."

Acacia drank the last of her wine and blew out the candle. It seemed that crying her heart out had a benefit—total exhaustion. And Sarah had eased her mind somehow. That feeling of being ready to burst was gone. As far as Noah was concerned? She wouldn't decide anything now.

* * *

Two weeks later, Noah pulled up in front of Acacia's house on Saturday afternoon. He sat in the driveway for a moment, anticipating the evening to come. For the first time, Jenny would be staying with Bobby while Acacia got away on her own. Noah was taking her to a weekly roping held at the San Antonio Rose Palace near Boerne, about twenty miles outside of San Antonio. The Palace was also the site of the George Strait Team Roping Classic, which he and Ronnie competed in every year. Today they were roping in one of the lighted outdoor arenas. Ronnie had hauled their horses so that Noah could pick up Acacia.

He'd agonized over whether to invite her. Bobby was a client, and she was his family. It was stretching the boundaries of his profession to see her this way. Yet he was powerless to stop. His need for her was a constant buzz in his head. He couldn't keep his thoughts away from her. He was lost.

She answered the door in full western dress, from the straw Stetson on her head to the silver barrel-racing buckle on her belt and the ostrich boots on her feet.

Grinning, he stepped into the house. "Maybe I should let you team up with Ronnie. You can probably out-rope me."

Laughing, she said, "I can rope, but I don't know about the rest. You and Ronnie are pretty damn fast."

She walked over and picked up her purse from the couch.

Noah couldn't take his eyes off her. She was just as sexy in her Wranglers today as she had been at the arena. Slender women often had flat butts, but Acacia had no such thing. Each firm cheek swelled out her back pockets in a delicious, enticing curve. And the T-shirt she wore hugged her slim waist. He would have a chore keeping his eyes to himself tonight, that was for sure.

When she turned around, he kept his gaze glued to hers. "You ready, then?" The smile on her cherry-red lips made him quiver.

She headed for the door. "Yep. Let's go."

* * *

Noah glanced at Acacia after he'd paid the parking fee. The lights from the arena cast her face in soft shadow, and her beauty was more striking than ever before. His chest tightened, and he returned his gaze to the dirt path leading to the trailer parking. How he wanted her. But what the hell could he do about it? There had to be an answer.

Ronnie had the horses unloaded when they arrived, and he nodded to Acacia. "Good to see you. How's Bobby?"

"He's enjoying his first evening on his own. Noah's friend Jenny is staying with him. I'm sure he's glad to get a break from me."

Ronnie smiled. "Happy you could come."

Noah saddled Red and slid the bridle over the halter. Leaving the halter on made it easy to tie him up when he wasn't being ridden. He glanced at Ronnie. "You sign in yet?"

He shook his head. "Just got here a few minutes ago."

"Okay. I'll walk Acacia over and take care of it. Get her settled in. Be back in a bit."

"Sounds good."

After he paid the entry fee and learned their place in the line-up, Noah took Acacia over to the gradually filling stands and found her a seat about twenty-five feet from the roping boxes. "This is a perfect spot. You'll catch all the action." He sat down next to her, enjoying the feeling of having a beautiful woman at his side. "I'll go fill Ronnie in. We're not up for a while, so I'll be back. Would you like a beer, or a hot dog, or anything else?"

"A beer would be great. Same as you drink is fine."

Grinning, he said, "Good choice. I'll be back in a few minutes." As he walked away, a thrill of anticipation ran through him. He had Acacia all to himself for the whole evening. Just as he'd figured, male heads turned wherever she went. She didn't even notice. He hadn't expected it to turn him on. He instantly felt protective, and yet proud. His primitive urges made him want to pull her to him and kiss her, marking his territory. He gusted out a breath. Acacia affected him in ways he'd never felt before. He was in for a wild ride with this woman. He couldn't keep his distance. Lord knew he'd tried. She was just too irresistible.

Ronnie was drinking a beer from the ice chest.

Noah grabbed one for himself and said, "It'll be a couple of hours. Lots of teams ahead of us."

Ronnie handed him cash for his part of the entry fee. "She looks beautiful tonight. You're a lucky man, my friend."

Noah blew out a breath. "She's gorgeous. I'm falling all over myself trying to act like I don't notice."

Ronnie shook his head. "I keep telling you, man, you shouldn't do that. The woman needs you."

Noah paused a moment, leaning against the truck before saying slowly, "Sometimes I think I pick up on her liking me. But then I'm not sure."

"This is her first night out, right? You need to show her a good time. She's waited two years for this."

"No pressure, then. Thanks." Noah pushed away from the truck. "I've got to get back. See you in about an hour, huh?"

He bought a beer and some nachos at the concession booth and headed to the stands. Acacia stood out from a distance. The dark curls falling around her shoulders contrasted with her pure, creamy-pale complexion, and her bright red T-shirt was like a neon sign.

She didn't see him coming, so he was able to study her. She seemed more animated tonight, more alive, as she studied the men warming up their horses in the arena. Her gaze flitted from one sight to another, and she smiled at the cowboys who cantered past her.

So this was who she was without the weight of Bobby on her shoulders. He had a glimpse of the happy, outgoing woman she must have been before the weight of her brother's care had settled on her.

As he approached, her smile broadened. "Hi."

He handed her the beer and set the nachos on her lap. "You didn't ask for these, but I've never known anyone who can resist rodeo nachos."

She laughed, and he was amazed at how it changed her face. This was the first real laugh he'd ever heard from her. It sent chills to his belly, exciting him.

Picking up one of the cheesy chips topped with a big jalapeno, she popped it into her mouth. "I won't be the first. I love them."

As he slid in next to her, his shoulder grazed hers. A thrill of joy raced through his veins. He'd wanted to be close to her for so long. Tonight was perfect. His upper arm rested against her, with just the lightest touch, and excitement sizzled through his chest.

She looked over at him and smiled. "I can't wait to watch you all rope. It's been years since I've been to a roping." She patted his knee, popping another nacho into her mouth. "Thank you so much for getting me out of the house."

Her touch was like a torch, lighting him on fire. How much more of this could he take? He set his beer on the bleacher and rubbed his palms up and down his thighs, looking out into the arena. Finally able to answer, he said, "I'm glad you said yes. It's a real treat for me to have someone in the stands."

Holding the nachos out, she grinned. "Want to share?"

His heart raced. She was so very beautiful. Would it hurt to forget, just this one night, that she was off-limits? He reached out to take a cheesy chip from the paper bowl she offered. Why not? Tonight, he'd forget she couldn't be his. He wouldn't feel guilty for enjoying her company, for admiring her beauty, her quick wit, her smile. Tonight, she would be his date.

The men left the arena. The roping was about to start. Acacia turned, her shoulder brushing his, and he welcomed the shudder of excitement that swept through him.

"Do you know a lot of the teams who're competing?" Acacia asked.

He answered, his voice surprising him with its steadiness. "New guys always show up, but we know quite a few of them. Everyone tries to attend the ropings that are close. Saves on time and gas money, though we do go farther afield once in a while."

After the presentation of the flag and a prayer, which the crowd stood for, the roping got underway. The first header only caught one horn and the nose. Though they were able to stretch the steer, the team suffered a time penalty. The second team ran their steer all the way to the end of the arena before roping and stretching him, so they also had a bad time. There were some fast times over the next hour, however.

Acacia clapped after a team put in a particularly quick time. "I still think you and Ronnie are better. I can't wait to see you guys out there."

Noah twisted his lips into a wry smile. "You're making me nervous. I'll mess up." He loved teasing her—bringing that beautiful, bright smile to her face. This animated, seemingly younger version of Acacia drew him in, made him want to do whatever it took to ensure she was always this happy.

Laughing, she said, "Oh, you will not. An old pro like you getting nervous because of little old me? I hardly think so."

He looked down at his hands and grinned. "You're right. I don't let pressure get to me much anymore." Still grinning, he caught her gaze and said, "But that doesn't mean there's no pressure."

Throwing her head back, she laughed some more.

He found himself staring. Her beauty mesmerized him. Her slender throat led his eyes down to the V of her neckline, where her breasts swelled enticingly. He snapped his eyes away.

Grinning, she said, "I'll be yelling for you. Listen for me."

Squeezing her shoulder, he said, "I need to go. Time I was on Red. There's an empty arena where we warm up. After that, Ronnie and I will hang out with the other teams and wait for our turn. Okay?"

"Sure."

What he wanted to do, what felt right to do now, was lean in and kiss her. He almost did. But he held back at the last second. The whole way over to the truck and trailer, he thought about what it would have felt like to kiss those red lips. What it would have been like to pull her into his arms and possess that sweet mouth. God, he was a wreck. This woman really had a hold on him.

Ronnie nodded as he walked up. "How is she?"

Noah shook his head and approached Red. "I'm so turned on when I'm with her, it's like I've been struck by lightning." He tightened Red's cinch and unhooked the lead rope. Swinging up into the saddle, he glanced at his best friend. "I want her more than I've ever wanted anybody." Picking up his rope, he said, "And not just the way you think. It's much more than that." Without thought, he started building his loop. "I'm lost. I don't know what to do."

Ronnie walked over and rested his hand on the horn of Noah's saddle, waiting for him to say more.

"I feel it coming, though. I'll do something. And I hope I can handle the consequences, partner." He nudged Red with his heels and moved off into the late evening shadows.

Noah had settled down by the time he'd warmed up Red and waited forty-five minutes behind the arena for their turn to rope. The team ahead of them was in the roping boxes. He and Ronnie had their loops ready.

Ronnie looked over at him and nodded. "You okay, buddy?"

"Yep. You?"

"Raring to go. Keep your head straight, now. No messing around, all right?"

In a moment, the head gate clanged, and the other team's horses burst out of the boxes, running down the steer in record time. Both ropers made their catch.

Ronnie shot his chin at Noah. "We can beat that. Just stay on your game."

Noah pressed his lips into a line. "Right."

The gate man opened the arena as the previous ropers left, and Ronnie and Noah entered, heading to the roping boxes. His name pealed out across the arena, and he grinned. That girl could holler. And, he was a little surprised to realize, that shout did make him a bit nervous. Damn.

Noah backed an excited Red into the far corner of the box, head pointing at the steer. This was what the horse lived for. The big animal quivered, anticipating the clang of the head gate.

Ronnie did the same with his horse in the other box.

Noah nodded. The head gate shot open, and the steer burst out of the chute. Red put Noah on him instantly. With a quick swing of his loop, he caught both horns. Turning Red and yanking the steer to the left allowed Ronnie to make a fast catch on the heels. Spinning their horses, the cowboys ran them backward, stretching the steer between them. The arena judge's flag flew on their time. And it was a fast one.

The audience clapped, and a loud "Woo-hoo" came from Acacia's direction. She was on her feet, jumping up and down and waving her hat. Lord, didn't she look cute.

He grinned and waved, and she whooped again.

The steer ran into the catch pen at the end of the arena with his rope still around its horns. The guy there pulled it off. Noah cantered down and retrieved it, thanking him.

He headed back to the truck and unsaddled Red, leaving the horse tied to the trailer. It'd be a while before the roping finished and the winning time was announced. Giving Red a final pat, he walked back toward the concessions and bought two more beers.

Acacia spotted him this time and stood as he approached. He caught his breath as he took in the vision she made. Biting the inside of his cheek to keep from smiling, he handed her one of the beers. "Thought you might need something cold after all that energy you put into yelling."

She laughed. "You all were great! I can't believe your time: 4.2 seconds! It's the best so far tonight."

He sat down and opened his beer. "Oh, there're some good teams still to rope yet. Don't get too excited."

Shaking her head, she said, "No, you handed in a super-fast time. I'd like to see someone beat it."

"Well, that's the best time we've had in a while. It's a big pot tonight. I hope we take it. My winnings always go into my business savings, and we've been winning a lot lately."

The stands were full now, so it was a tight squeeze when she sat down. Her thigh rested against his, and their hips touched. Raw energy buzzed through him. He wanted to wrap his arm around her and pull her close, breathe in the sweet smell of her hair and kiss the pale skin at her temple. Clenching his eyes tight, he turned his head. *Come on, man. Come on. Chill the hell out.* He gulped some beer and watched the next team of ropers race after their steer.

Catching her out of the corner of his eye, he saw that she appeared unfazed by their close proximity. Was he the only one going crazy here? The cowboys coiled their ropes and left the arena as the next team came in. These guys were usually in the money. Noah pointed. "They're fast. Keep an eye on their time."

Acacia patted his knee. "You have nothing to worry about."

Lord, the knee again? He could still feel the faint trace of her fingertips. His energy ramped even higher, and he bounced his heel up and down, jiggling his leg. The cowboys backed into the roping boxes and settled for a moment, then the header nodded. The steer exploded out of the chute. The horses gave chase. The header quickly caught both horns, then the heeler snapped up the back legs. They stretched the steer between them, and the judge flagged the time. It was fast, but not fast enough.

Acacia clapped her hands and leaned over, giving his shoulder a playful bump. "I told you. Not a chance."

He loved it. Loved her playfulness, the excitement in her eyes, and the fact that she was living out loud for the first time since he'd met her. This Acacia had been driven so deep by worry and burden that he'd never imagined she was there. He pulled her to him, squeezing her gently, then releasing her. He didn't dare hold her any longer for fear of doing more.

Acacia stared up at him, her eyes gone soft and deep.

He matched her gaze, allowing his feelings to show.

She reached out and touched his cheek, then turned her attention to the arena.

* * *

They left the Rose Palace after midnight. Noah and Ronnie had won. Acacia was ecstatic, though she seemed tired now that the exhilaration of the night was over. Noah's arm rested on the center console and, on impulse, he reached over and picked up her hand. Lacing his fingers through hers, he said, "I want to say something, and don't take it wrong. I'd like to pay for Jenny's services tonight. I feel like if I ask you to go somewhere, I should be the one to take care of her. You can pay her when you go someplace, but I don't want you worrying about coming up with money if I ask you to go somewhere with me. Would you let me do that?"

She frowned. "That's not necessary. Of course Sarah said that she'd pay for a sitter, but I don't feel comfortable with that. I'm glad that she bugged me, though, until I actually found Jenny, thanks to you."

"Well it might not be necessary, but I'd sure feel better about paying. I want you spending your money on you and Bobby. Would you please allow me to do this?"

She looked out the window for a bit, then turned back. "Okay, that's fair, I guess. Thank you."

"No, thank you. I appreciate it because I'd like to ask you to do things once in a while and not feel guilty about it." He squeezed her fingers. "You doing okay? Tired?"

Squeezing his hand back, she leaned her head against the seat. "I'm a good kind of tired. I had a wonderful time tonight."

He kept his eyes on the steady I-10 traffic. She didn't mind him holding her hand. In fact, it appeared she welcomed it. The link through their fingers was strong, as though their energies had intertwined. Something of her flowed into him. He wasn't imagining it. The feeling was solid and warm and beautiful. Stroking her thumb with his, he said, "It meant a lot to me having you there. Did I tell you that you make a great cheering section?"

She chuckled. "No."

"Oh, well, you do. I could hear you screaming as I came into the arena."

She chuckled again and yawned quietly. Closing her eyes, she snuggled down and said, "Well, my guys always know I have their back. I make sure of that."

Noah faced his side window to hide his huge grin. So he was her guy, huh? That had a nice ring to it. But she appeared to be falling asleep. She'd probably say anything in the shape she was in. Still, her guy? He liked it. Squeezing her hand softly, he silently wished her sweet dreams.

* * *

Acacia lay in bed Sunday morning still under the awful spell of her dream. It had started out so wonderfully. She and Noah were married, living on a cattle ranch, and she had a baby boy. The child meant everything to them. Holding the infant in her arms, she crooned to him, waiting for Noah to come in for the evening. Then he walked through the door and swooped the child up, cuddling him. That was when she knew. Her other child was missing. Screaming, she raced through the house, looking in closets and behind furniture. Where was he? Had he somehow gotten out of the house? Had he been stolen?

Heart hammering, she woke—and realized her missing child was Bobby. Her dream was about abandoning him. She turned over and buried her face in the pillow. Her subconscious mind must know something she hadn't admitted to herself. Was she considering doing that? How could she? It went against everything she believed in. Shaken, she slid out of bed and started a shower. She wouldn't desert her twin. Her subconscious had it wrong. Yet, as she stepped into the hot running water, a small part of her was afraid she might.

* * *

Monday afternoon, Acacia took a sip of wine and settled deeper into the cushions of her chair. She loved that her house was built so that the back porch was shaded from the summer sun in the afternoons. High on its stand, the oscillating fan blew over her shoulder and lifted loose tendrils of her hair.

Once Bobby's morning bath was over, she'd had a quiet day. After fixing an easy lunch, she'd gone outside, sifting through memories of Noah and their time together Saturday night. He'd touched her, even hugged her. If she closed her eyes right now, she'd feel those touches again. Exquisitely gentle. Elusively quick. She'd wondered at the time just what he'd meant by them. Then he'd opened himself wide, let her see his soul. She'd known what he wanted.

Taking another sip of wine, she let her gaze wander over her pots of herbs. Noah had been so brave. He'd really put it all out there for her to see. She hadn't been as honest. She'd been afraid. Scared that if she let go, let him see how much she yearned for him, that there'd be no turning back. She hadn't been ready for that. She still wasn't anywhere near geared up for the risk of caring for him.

She laid her phone down on the table and dialed Sarah as she took another sip of wine. She'd never smoked, but that didn't stop her from thinking how much she might like to whenever she felt like this. Looking at her hand wrapped around the stemware, she imagined a cigarette held between her first two fingers. It would be so soothing to slip that cigarette into her mouth and take a long, relaxing drag.

Sarah answered. "Hey, you. What's up?"

"Nothing. You busy?"

"Just got home. I have time to talk, though. I did the crock pot thing this morning, so dinner's taken care of."

Her friend's footsteps tapped in the background, most likely headed for the bedroom. "I hired Jenny to stay with Bobby Saturday evening and went to a roping with Noah."

"What? That's awesome! Give me the details."

Sarah's shoes clumped as she kicked them off, and there were more muffled sounds as she undressed.

"Noah and Ronnie had the best time of the night. Took home the winnings. I told Noah they should go pro, but he wants to focus on his physical therapy. Did you know he plans to open his own therapy business?"

"Really? The man has ambitions. I like that."

Hesitantly, Acacia told her friend how Noah had seemed different, more attentive, how he'd touched her, even wrapped his arm around her briefly, and about the look. "His eyes were so full. He wanted me to see how much he cares, how much he wanted me. Sarah, I didn't know what to do."

"Whoa, he's thrown his cards on the table. It's your play now."

"I know, and, I'm not sure I want to. I have to go all in or fold, and I'm too scared to do either. You remember how I was when Johnny left, don't you? And I still had Bobby and Mom and Dad to worry about. I don't ever want to go through that kind of hurt again. I don't think I can."

Sarah hurried to reassure her. "Honey, I remember how bad you were. I was scared I was losing you. I think the last thing Noah would want is to put more pressure on you. Don't decide anything now. If he cares about you, he'll wait until the time is right."

She sighed, knowing her friend made sense. That was the kind of guy Noah was. "Sarah, you always know what to say."

Sarah chuckled. "It's one of my many talents. You cheer up now. You're a lucky girl to have that man caring about you. It'll all turn out fine."

Chapter Five

Wednesday evening, Noah handed Ronnie a beer and settled beside him in a cedar log rocking chair on the long, shady front porch of his ranch house.

Ronnie took a swallow and thrust his chin at Noah. "How's Acacia? Seemed like she was having a good time Saturday."

Noah scratched his cheek and stared off into the barn pasture, irritated at the scratchy sound his fingernails made on his five-o'clock shadow. "Yeah, she seemed to have fun."

"Uh-huh. But?"

He turned to Ronnie. "She's holding back. I'm not sure why. I can tell she likes me."

His friend took another swallow of his beer. "Huh."

"Maybe I should respect her holding back. I mean, I get it. I worry, too. I look at Bobby and I think of Joe and I think, *What am I doing taking all that on?*" Noah took a long swallow of beer. "Then I think about letting her go, and I can't. I just can't, Ronnie."

His friend laughed. "You got it bad, buddy."

Noah stared at his boots. "Don't I know it."

"Partner, she's got a lot to consider. Bobby depends on her. And she's a good woman. It's why you care about her so much. Don't push it. She'll figure this out."

Noah nodded slowly, chewing the inside of his cheek.

Ronnie squinted an eye at him. "Are you sure you've thought this through? Say somehow this all works out. Are you sure you want to take on the care of an invalid for the rest of your life? You know how caring for Joe dragged your momma down. Do you want to see that happen to the woman you love? Do you need the kind of responsibility that comes with caring for a severely disabled individual?"

Noah sighed. "Like I said, I've thought of that. And it's a lot. But there will be two of us sharing the burden. My mom only had me to help her, and I was a boy. My dad never helped out with Joe. Looking back, I don't know why, either. I never thought to ask. It just was."

"This will affect everything you do. And what about when you have kids? Imagine Acacia taking care of babies and having Bobby to care for, too. Think about all of it, Noah, before you jump into this," Ronnie said.

Noah finished his beer and set the can on the wooden porch. "I hear what you're saying. But I can't get her out of my mind. I'm always thinking about her, wondering what she's doing, how Bobby is. It's kind of taken me over." He furrowed his brow. "I like thinking about her, though."

Ronnie downed the last of his beer and stood. "Like I said, you got it bad, buddy. Just be careful, okay? I wouldn't want you to get hurt."

* * *

Thursday evening, Noah finished strapping Bobby's wheelchair down and shut the sliding door on the van. The three of them were headed out for pizza. He rode shotgun while Acacia drove. After spending that evening with her at the roping, she'd been all he could think about. It had driven him crazy, and he'd given up on being professional. He'd had to see her again. When he'd called to ask her and Bobby out for pizza and she'd agreed, he'd felt so relieved. He was completely under her spell.

She pulled away from the curb. "Where are we going, sir?"

"Do you have a favorite place?"

She grinned. "We love any kind of pizza, so you choose."

"You're making this too easy." He gave her directions and sat back, watching her competent handling of the large vehicle.

A few minutes later, they stopped at a red light in a busy intersection. Noah turned around to speak to Bobby. "You pretty hungry, big guy? I sure am."

Bobby nodded. "Noah, I'm hu-hungry."

He reached around and patted Bobby's knee, turning back in time to notice the light turn green.

Acacia eased off the brake and entered the intersection.

With a deafening *boom*, a pickup truck slammed into the van on the driver's side.

Acacia flew sideways, constrained by her seatbelt and airbag from hitting into the passenger window as the van slewed toward the side of the road.

Noah, his head pounding from the force of the deployed airbag and impacting the door, jerked his seat belt off and scrambled to reach Bobby. Having taken the brunt of the collision, the center of the van was a mess. Crumpled steel from the door panel intruded into the space where Bobby should have been. Broken glass lay everywhere. His wheelchair tilted crazily.

Bobby hung limply over the side of his chair, yelling in fear.

Acacia jerked frantically at her own belt, which jammed from the impact.

Noah reached Bobby, wrapping his arm around him and supporting his weight as he called 911.

Bobby calmed down some.

Acacia pulled free.

Noah looked behind him, trying to assess her condition. "You hurt?"

"My leg. The door got it. But I'm okay. What about Bobby?"

"I don't know. His upper harness came loose. Let's trade places, if you can without hurting your leg. Support Bobby and his chair. I can't imagine why the thing hasn't fallen over yet. I'll open the door. We can get a better look, and I need to check and see if the van is leaking anything dangerous."

With some effort, Acacia climbed over, and Noah was able to force the opposing door open and crawl out of the van. The tie-down braces had broken, and the only thing holding the wheelchair partially upright was the wreckage of the other side door on the drivers' side of the vehicle.

Bobby whimpered helplessly. Sounds dinged from the dash and engines gunned as cars pulled around the crashed vehicles and left the intersection.

A couple walked up. "Can I do anything?" the man asked.

Noah peered over his shoulder. "Would you check on who-ever is in that truck? Find out if they're injured?"

"Sure."

Bobby had started crying again, though more quietly this time. "My head hurts, Noah. I want out. Help me, Noah."

He couldn't stand hearing Bobby cry. He wanted to take him out right then. It might be as simple as taking off the re-maining restraints in his wheelchair and pulling him out, but he wasn't an EMT. He shouldn't do anything. He had to be patient.

"I'm right here, Bobby. I'll take care of you. People are coming to help pull you out. They know how to do it right, and I don't." Noah relieved Acacia, wrapping his arms around Bobby and supporting his weight, letting Bobby's head rest on his shoulder. "Is that better, buddy?"

Bobby sniffed. "Yeah. But I want out."

"Sure you do. We'll have you out real soon."

In a minute, Bobby said, "I want pizza, Noah. Do the pe-people have pizza?"

Noah smiled. "Sorry, Bobby, they won't be bringing pizza. But I'll make sure you eat some pizza as soon as I can, okay?"

Bobby sighed. "Okay, Noah. Can I get out now?"

"They'll be here in a little bit, Bobby. Then we'll get you out."

"Okay."

Acacia took over while he checked under the van for fluid leakage. She entertained Bobby by telling him stories about the Blue Heeler cowdog they grew up with on the ranch. Then she explained what would happen with his EMS helpers and about going to the emergency room.

The wail of a siren sounded a few blocks away as Noah returned to relieve Acacia. She got out of the vehicle to stretch her injured leg, and he patted Bobby's arm. "Hear that? It sounds like your red car. That's the people who're coming to help you. We'll be out of here in a little while."

The EMTs were professional and kind. Even so, Bobby cried when Noah released his hold. The EMT who replaced Noah held Bobby in his arms and reassured him that everything would be fine while the other EMT assessed the situation.

Just then a firetruck arrived, and two more EMTs got out. It would take more than two people to bring Bobby out safely since the wheelchair was firmly a part of the wreckage.

A tow truck came to pull the damaged truck away from the van.

The driver of the truck hadn't worn his seat belt, and he had facial lacerations as well as other injuries. Another EMS vehicle arrived on the scene to care for him.

Noah frowned and glanced around. Where was Acacia? Pulse racing, he walked to the other side of the van. There she was, head bowed, hunched over with her arms across her chest. He hurried to her.

"Are you all right? I was worried. I couldn't find you." A wide band of blood had run down the leg of her pants. "You're hurt. We need you looked at right now." He reached for her, yet she still didn't look at him, and he realized she was crying.

He clasped her arm, tilting her chin, insisting that she look at him. "What is it? What's wrong?"

She covered her face with her hands. "The wreck was my fault. I should have seen that truck coming at us. Bobby could have terrible things wrong with him, and I'm to blame."

Noah pulled her into his arms, pressing her damp face against his shirt. "Shush, shush, you weren't at fault. That bastard ran a red light. You had the right of way." He cupped her head in his hand and kissed her temple. "You're not to blame for this. We'll deal with whatever happens to Bobby together, all right? Now, come on. Let's go find out how they're doing getting him out of the van."

He slid his arm around her shoulders as they headed back around the vehicle. She seemed so damn fragile, as though every spark of strength had gone out of her. And she was limping.

As they approached, they saw one EMT who wasn't actively working with Bobby. Noah drew Acacia alongside the woman. "Do you think you could take a look at this leg?"

Acacia pressed her lips together. Noah knew stubborn when he saw it. She shook her head. "I'm fine. I don't want to leave Bobby right now."

Noah was firm. "I'll watch over him. You're all bloody. Let the lady check you over and see if the wound is serious. Please, do it for me, okay?"

Grudgingly, and with a backward glance into the van at her brother, she followed the woman to the ambulance.

He spent the time she was gone giving as much information as he knew about Bobby to another EMT. He also called a cab.

Ten minutes later, once the EMTs had finally gotten Bobby out and onto a stretcher, Acacia came back. He turned to her. "That was fast. How did it go?"

"I explained that I don't have insurance, so she put some butterfly bandages on the cut and said if the soreness doesn't go away in a day or so I need to have my leg X-rayed. She didn't even charge me. Wrote it up as a community assist."

Her eyes teared up again. "Look at this van. What will I do? I still owe so much on the damn thing—I'm probably upside down on my loan. And Bobby will need another wheelchair. How will I even bring him home from the hospital?" She squeezed her eyes shut and turned away from him.

He rested his hands on her shoulders. "I told Ronnie I'd call as soon as I knew which hospital we were going to. He'll meet me there with his ranch truck. It's old, but it works fine. You can use it to run errands until you figure out what to do. I'll find you a wheelchair you can use temporarily. Just don't worry about that stuff for now. We'll get through this one thing at a time, okay?"

She nodded and scrubbed her cheeks dry. "Thanks."

As the EMTs rolled by with Bobby, she stopped them. "Can I ride with him?"

The man shook his head. "Sorry, no, ma'am. Against regs."

Acacia grimaced. "He's a veteran. We need to take him to the SAMMC emergency room. I'll meet you there." She took Bobby's hand and walked along beside him as they moved on toward the ambulance. "Bobby, these nice men will drive you to the hospital. It'll be fun. You'll get to hear the siren, like your red car. I'll meet you there, okay? You'll see me there."

Bobby's eyes grew wide. "No. I don't want to go." He cried. "Come with me, 'Cacia."

She motioned to the EMTs. "Please stop." Hugging Bobby, she kissed him and caressed his cheek. "I'll be right behind you, honey. Don't worry, you're safe."

Bobby cried harder as they loaded him into the ambulance.

Acacia turned to Noah, tears filling her eyes and spilling down her cheeks. "He's scared. I wish I could ride with him. How far away is the cab?"

"I'm not sure. I should have called Uber. Then I could check."

Right after the ambulance finally headed out of the intersection, their cab drove up. Noah helped Acacia in, then climbed in himself. "SAMMC emergency, please."

Noah spied a box of Kleenex in the front seat. He pulled a couple out and handed them to Acacia.

She wiped her eyes and then blew her nose.

He slid his arm around her shoulders and held her close. As he dialed Ronnie on his cell, he said, "We'll be there in a bit, Acacia. Why don't you shut your eyes and try to relax?"

Ronnie answered his phone, and Noah told him where they were going. After returning the phone to his shirt pocket, he reached out and pulled a few strands of hair away from Acacia's face.

She opened her eyes. Worry and fear stared back at him.

He squeezed her a little and leaned in, kissing her temple. Holding her, reassuring her, seemed so perfect. Like she was a part of him. "You're all right. I've got this. Relax."

She closed her eyes again and sighed.

She appeared so lost. He'd do whatever it took to help her and make sure Bobby was taken care of.

Twenty minutes later, he paid the cabbie as they arrived at SAMMC Emergency. The place was a huge complex, and he was glad he hadn't had to find his way here on his own. He clasped Acacia's hand as they walked in through the emergency room doors.

She strode up to the desk. "We're here for my brother, Robert Richards. He was brought in by ambulance. I need to see him."

The woman checked her computer. "He's in triage. It'll be a few minutes."

Acacia bit her lip. Poor Bobby. "My brother has the mind of a small child. He's been in a car wreck, and he's scared to death. Is there any way I can get back there immediately?"

The woman shook her head. "I'm sorry. Let me call someone. We'll get you back there."

"Thank you. I appreciate it."

A minute later, the double doors to the back opened, and a young man stepped out. "Richards?"

Acacia rushed to his side. "That's us. Thank you for coming."

They walked down a corridor to a large area lined on all four sides with glassed-in rooms. Bobby's cries rang out loudly from one of them.

"No! No! I want 'Cacia!"

She called out, "I'm here, Bobby," and headed in the direction of his voice.

He yelled, "'Cacia! 'Cacia!"

She walked through the open glass doors. "I'm here, honey. You're okay. I'm here." She leaned over the bed rail, hugging him and stroking his hair.

The nurse attending Bobby gave them a relieved smile. "I'm glad you got here. He's been really worried. Hasn't wanted us to touch him. EMTs said he cried a lot on the way here. The doctor should be in here in a few minutes, and he's ordered some tests. You being here will make that go much smoother."

It was Noah's turn to give Bobby a hug. "Hey there, buddy. You need to be a big man this evening, okay? The doctors have to do lots of stuff to make sure you're not hurt. We can't go home until they're finished. You want to go home, don't you?"

"I want to go ho-me, Noah."

"Sure you do. But you have to help the doctors first, buddy. Will you do that for me?"

Bobby sighed deeply and closed his eyes. "Yeah, Noah. But I don't like it here."

"I'll be with you, Bobby. You're safe. Acacia will be here, too."

He kept his eyes closed. "Okay. I'm hungry. Do they have pizza?"

Noah brushed his hair from his forehead. "I don't think so, buddy. I don't think the doctor wants you to eat right now, either."

"Okay."

He was falling asleep. The poor guy had been overwhelmed and upset since the accident. Crying had really worn him out. Noah held out his hand for Acacia's purse and motioned for her to sit in the chair.

"What'll you do?" she asked.

"I'm fine to stand. I don't have a banged-up leg." Despite the upset and strain, she looked incredibly beautiful. It took all his restraint to keep from taking her into his arms and comforting her.

With obvious reluctance, she sat down, keeping her sore leg extended in front of her.

The nurse had left the room, so it was just the two of them. He set her purse on the countertop and dimmed the lights, then stood beside her, leaning his shoulders against the wall. Some of the tension of the past hour eased out of his system.

The nurse came back in, moving quietly when she saw Bobby sleeping. She entered some information into the computer and asked Acacia for Bobby's military ID card. Then she began softly asking questions about Bobby's medical history, his medications, and the accident. The intake went on and on. Acacia was very patient. She'd obviously been through these procedures with Bobby before.

Noah had turned his ringer off when Bobby had fallen asleep, so when Ronnie called, his phone vibrated. Squeezing Acacia's shoulder, he pointed to the door and left.

His friend stood near the waiting-room door.

Ronnie gave him a hug, holding him for an extra beat or two. "How's Bobby? How's Acacia doing?"

They sat down in two of the waiting-room chairs. Noah shook his head. "Don't know anything yet. Doc hasn't been in. Guess Bobby cried all the way over here. Poor guy was scared to death. Acacia's tough, but she's real worried. Ronnie, we got hit hard. The wreck totaled the van, and the truck hit right where Bobby's wheelchair was. He could be hurt bad, and he'd never know." Noah leaned his elbows on his knees and put his head in his hands, talking through his fingers. "Poor guy. He just can't catch a break."

After a moment, he sat up straight. "Thanks for letting us borrow the truck. It's a big help. Bobby may not go home tonight, so I'll probably drive it home. I have to round up a wheelchair for him first thing tomorrow. Acacia'll have to call her insurance in the morning, too. She'll need to buy another van."

Ronnie slapped his shoulder and gave it a squeeze. "Yeah, but she's got you. She'll be all right. I have to go. Karen's outside in the car. The baby fell asleep. She said to tell you she loves you."

"Same here." He hugged Ronnie again before he left.

When Noah walked back into Bobby's room, Acacia had her head resting on the wall and her eyes closed. He eased the glass door shut and leaned against the wall beside her again. She looked done in, and the worry on her face went straight to his heart. Bobby was still asleep. The nurse had gone, so maybe they could all rest a while before the doctor came in. He leaned his head back and closed his eyes.

About fifteen minutes later, the doctor slid the door open and rushed in, followed by their nurse, who flipped on the lights. The doctor reached out his hand to Acacia. "Hi, I'm Dr. Ramsey. I'll be managing Bobby's care this evening." He shook Noah's hand as well.

Noah offered, "I'm Noah Rowden, Bobby's physical therapist."

The doctor drew his brows together in confusion.

Noah clarified. "I was with them when the accident happened. We were going out for pizza."

The doctor nodded. "Oh, right. So I take it this was a pretty serious accident?"

Acacia answered. "Very." She went on to describe the damage to the van and how it had affected Bobby.

Dr. Ramsey walked over and gently patted Bobby's cheek to wake him as he continued. "Of course, with Bobby's situation, we've got to be entirely sure he hasn't suffered any injury. I've ordered a CAT scan and scheduled an MRI. We'll do blood work, and I want some chest X-rays as well."

Bobby opened his eyes and squinted at the doctor.

Dr. Ramsey introduced himself and peered through his ophthalmoscope into Bobby's eyes. "I think it's a good idea to keep Bobby overnight for observation. Sometimes it takes a while for injuries to show up. I've already requested a room for him." He put on his stethoscope and listened to Bobby's heart and lungs. Smiling at him, he turned to Acacia. "Do you have any questions?" Pulling the sheet down, he began examining Bobby. The nurses had cut his clothes off before Acacia and Noah arrived, so he was naked under the sheet.

Acacia stood and leaned over the bed to get a better view of any possible injuries. His hip was already starting to bruise. She pointed at it.

Dr. Ramsey nodded. "We'll check all that. Let's hope it's nothing serious. There's no point in getting worried until all the test results are in. His left lung sounds a little congested, by the way. He took a hard bump." Dr. Ramsey walked over to Acacia's side of the bed. Bobby's rib area was discolored. "Yeah, we'll check all this out. See what we're dealing with." He glanced at Acacia. "Are you staying with him tonight? I can get you a sleeping chair in his room."

"Oh, please. That would help a lot. I'll be here."

"His room should be ready by the time his tests are done."

After the doctor finished his exam, Acacia helped the nurse put a gown on Bobby.

A few minutes later, the nurse brought in a chair for Noah. "It'll be a long night. I thought you could use this."

Noah let fly with one of his slick rodeo-cowboy smiles, nearly causing the poor woman to swoon. "Thanks so much. I really appreciate it."

After she left, Acacia rolled her eyes at him, and he grinned.

Scooting his chair close to hers, he pressed his shoulder against her. "Lean on me and get some shut-eye. The nurse was right. And don't worry about Bobo. I'll go feed him and let him out. Tonight will be a long night." His pulse quickened in anticipation.

Acacia looked at him, and he picked out a few things in her eyes. She was thanking him. And she was tired. And there was a spark of something else. Maybe she wanted him some, too.

He smiled to himself and leaned his head back. It might be a long night, but, sitting here beside his girl, it would be a good night, too.

* * *

Acacia took a sip of iced tea and closed her eyes, thankful for the sanctuary offered by her shady back porch. She'd had a hell of a two weeks. Her parents had come down as soon as she'd called them about the accident. They'd co-signed on the loan for her new van, which was the only way she could qualify quickly. It would take weeks to settle with the insurance on the old one. It took time to install a Tommy Lift for Bobby's wheelchair, too. She couldn't wait weeks to buy a new van, then wait more time for the lift installation. Even so, it had been just yesterday that Noah had helped her retrieve her new van with its wheelchair lift from the dealership.

What would she have done without Noah? He'd been there for everything. He'd found her a loaner wheelchair in a size that fit Bobby the very next day after the accident. That was a miracle in itself. Then he'd arranged to borrow a van from one of his other clients to take Bobby home from SAMMC since an ambulance ride home wasn't a paid benefit. It sounded ridiculous, but that was the way things worked.

Bobby wouldn't have therapy for a couple more weeks, as he'd suffered a fractured rib in the crash. Thank God that was the only thing that had been wrong. It could have been so much worse. She'd been terrified when his upper harness had failed, allowing his body to flail about in the wreck.

Noah had still come regularly to visit Bobby, however. With her permission, one of the first things he'd done was bring pizza for dinner. Noah and Bobby looked forward to seeing each other and, she had to admit, she wanted to see Noah, too. The handsome cowboy had won a solid place in her thoughts—stealing her away while she washed dishes or when she was alone on the porch.

He'd been so good to her. Yet it was more than that. His touch thrilled her, sent hot waves of desire flooding her body. She couldn't deny it anymore. She wanted him. Wanted his touch, his soft kisses, wanted his arms around her. And the accident had shown her that she needed this man who had come into their lives and turned them upside down. She had yet to come to terms with the downside, though. What would she do when he bailed?

Chapter Six

Acacia swore softly. Her hands were shaking so badly she couldn't slide the back of her earring on. Noah had asked her to dinner, and he'd be here any minute. The thought sent her heart skittering again. Finally settling her earring in place, she strode to the mirror. God, she hoped this dress wasn't too much. The royal-blue sheath came to mid-thigh. She'd bought it on a whim before her wedding, hoping it would catch Johnny's eye on their honeymoon, and she'd never worn it. Slipping on her red heels, she grabbed a matching evening bag and walked into the living room.

Jenny grinned. "You're stunning. I love your hair up like that, and the curls you left around your face are perfect. Very sexy."

Heat rose to Acacia's cheeks. God, would Noah think she was trying to be sexy? Her other choices had been sundresses or her black funeral dress. The doorbell rang. "Thank you, Jenny. You're sweet." She headed for the door, a little unsure of her footing in the four-inch heels after years of wearing flats.

She opened the door and moved aside. "Come in."

He stood for a few seconds, his gaze traveling over her. "You look beautiful tonight, Acacia. I'm a lucky man."

She smiled, thrilling at the rasp in his husky voice. Speaking of beautiful—Noah was a perfect specimen of male fitness in pressed Wranglers and a stiffly ironed black shirt.

He removed his hat as he stepped inside, his bootheels echoing on the ceramic tile of the entryway.

She noted the large, shiny new trophy buckle he wore on his belt, then bit her lip, wondering what she was doing with her gaze down there.

Bobby called out, "Noah, hi, Noah."

Noah walked over and gave him a hug. "Hey, bud. You doing okay?"

"Yeah, Jenny's here. She's my friend."

The pretty young woman grinned. "We'll be fine. You two go have fun."

Noah turned to Acacia. "You ready?"

She clutched her purse tighter. That killer smile of his had her melting already. How could she handle a whole night alone with him? She'd be putty in his hands. "All set."

He placed his hand lightly at her waist, sending shivers up her back. God, this man aroused everything female in her. She stepped across the threshold and said a prayer to resist the wantonness now coiled in her belly. For two years this need had been sublimated by the necessity of caring for a desperately wounded soldier. And tonight, it wanted free. Could she control it? Or would it escape its hiding place to do what it willed? Gripping the railing, she started down the ramp.

Once on their way, Noah told her where he'd made reservations, adding, "I love Boudro's, but I haven't been in a while. Have you ever eaten there?"

Whew. A safe conversation. She shook her head. "This really isn't where I planned on living. I'm in San Antonio so that Bobby can be close to SAMMC. And he's been injured as long as I've been here, so I don't go out much."

Noah reached across and clasped her hand. "Well, we need to remedy that. Boudro's has great Texas-style food, and I reserved a table on the Riverwalk. The patio isn't fancy, but it's fun to people-watch." He grinned. "And they have a great wine selection. I know you'll appreciate that."

"It sounds wonderful." Turning to the window, she closed her eyes. Johnny had never held her hand, something she hadn't even realized until Noah had started doing it. Holding his hand was like having a pipeline straight to his heart. He squeezed gently to show he cared, pulled her nearer when he needed intimacy, clasped firmly when he was concerned. His openness was one of the things that drew her to him. He held nothing back.

As if reading her thoughts, he pressed her fingers. "Tired?"

"No, just relaxing and thinking. Have I said thanks, by the way, for taking me away for the night? This is such a treat."

"It's a treat for me too. I never go anywhere except for ropings on Saturdays."

She frowned slightly. "I know this is none of my business, but why doesn't a man like you date?"

Grinning, he said, "A man like me, huh?"

She scowled mockingly. "You know what I mean. You could choose from a whole crowd of women. How come you don't have a girlfriend—or a wife, for that matter?"

He looked away for a few seconds, and then returned his gaze to her. "I've dated. And there was someone, once. She wasn't cut out for settling down, as I found out. I didn't like how that felt. Anyway, I'm busy with my work, saving for my business. I have the livestock and roping. It's not like I sit around missing having a woman in my life."

She let that sink in. He'd had some bumps and bruises along the way, too, then. Changing the subject, she asked, "Is Ronnie married?"

"He is. Has a new baby. She's four months old. Marriage and that little girl have made him a mighty happy man."

When he squeezed her hand, she smiled. "It sounds like a wonderful life." She leaned her head back on the seat, comfortable in the silence between them. That was one of the best things about Noah. He was fine with quiet, too.

She wanted to memorize these moments tonight, to gather them into a treasure chest and seal them inside. Tomorrow, when she awoke lonely and hopeless, she'd open her secret hoard and relive her time with this caring man who looked at her with such want in his eyes.

* * *

Boudro's was everything Noah had promised. The relaxed atmosphere on the Riverwalk and simple dining arrangements went a long way toward making Acacia comfortable. After all, it had been ages since she'd eaten out—and a lot longer since her last date. And this was a date, right?

Noah held her chair. The simple, gentlemanly act sent goosebumps rippling up her arms.

"I love the Riverwalk. Have you ever been down here at night?" he asked.

She wrinkled her nose. "I kind of hate to admit this after living here for two years, but no, I haven't. The lights are all so beautiful, and I can't believe the barges. This is wonderful."

As Noah sat down, their server came, and they ordered drinks. Noah picked up his menu. "I figured you liked Mexican food after noticing you grew jalapenos on your porch. They have a lot of it on their menu here, among other things."

She was having a hard time focusing on the words in front of her. Noah was so handsome sitting across the table, and yet his gentleness was evident, too. He excited her, pulled at her, made her want to tug him into her arms and kiss him until she hadn't a breath of air left in her lungs.

The server brought their drinks. Her hand shook as she reached for her wine and downed a long swallow. This response of hers to Noah was so unlike her. Surely a glass of wine would calm her? Scanning the menu, she quickly made a choice and took a couple more swallows of wine.

She closed her menu and glanced at Noah.

He was staring at her. "Everything okay?"

The wine. Of course. She'd practically guzzled it. "Yes. I guess I'm just thirsty."

"Do you need some water?"

"That would be great." She steeled her expression into a smile. *No, I need the rest of my damn wine. I need my hands to stop shaking. I need to get my shit together before I end up making a fool of myself.*

The waiter came and took their dinner orders, and Noah asked for another round of drinks and some water.

She finished off her first glass of wine quickly as he talked about his herd of Black Angus cattle.

She smiled and took a calming breath. "Do you buy your roping steers at auction, or do you know someone around here who has them?"

"A little of both, I guess. I keep twenty steers on hand. Once they get head shy, I sell them. If I can't keep the pen full from auction, I can call some guys. Being this close to Mexico is a bonus. Mexican cattle are cheaper and have better roping horns."

This was another thing she liked about Noah. He enjoyed talking rodeo and ranching. She loved her western lifestyle and had missed having someone to talk with about it.

The waiter served them, and Noah kept up an easy conversation.

She sipped her wine, enjoying his deep voice, his husky laugh, and the gentle way his eyes caressed her when he asked a question. She finished the last of her dinner with her heart back to its normal beat and her hands steady.

Noah laid down his napkin. "How would you like to listen to some great jazz and blues before we head home?"

Her pulse sped up. Jazz and the blues were music's languages of the heart. Was it a good idea to sit next to this gorgeous man and listen to music that spoke to a body that way?

Noah pressed. "You'll love it. I promise."

Why shouldn't she go? Just this once. What could it hurt to enjoy this one night and forget her responsibilities back at home?

He reached across the table and clasped her hand. "You won't regret it."

Laughing, she said, "Okay. It sounds perfect."

He stood and walked around to help her with her chair. "Good choice. We should be able to grab a seat since it's a weeknight. Weekends, we'd have a hard time getting in. The place is called Jazz, TX, and it's in the cellar at the old Pearl Brewery."

With his hand resting gently at her waist, he escorted her through the evening Riverwalk crowd toward the parking lot.

Her belly fluttered at his touch. She remembered the hot way he'd looked at her at the house, and her lips twitched upward. It was so damned good to be out tonight, on the arm of a sexy man, about to hear beautiful, lazy music in a dark room with nothing on her mind but having a wonderful time.

Noah pulled her in close as the way ahead got more crowded.

Hot blood rushed through her. Noah had already played his hand. It was her turn to lay down her cards. Sliding an arm around his waist, she leaned her head into his shoulder. Bring it on, blues.

* * *

Noah spotted two chairs at a table in the back corner farthest from the stage. Perfect. He led Acacia around the other tables, most full of customers. The club was dark, and the band was playing. Leaning in close, he asked as quietly as he could, "What would you like to drink?"

The waitress came, and he gave their order. He settled back in his chair and looked at Acacia as she watched the woman crooning on stage.

The music swayed through the shadows, easing him into the mood the blues always created. He seldom brought women here with him. In fact, he couldn't remember the last time he had. The blues loosened him up, dropped his walls like nothing else ever did.

But he wanted to share it with Acacia. He didn't really understand it except that he needed her close. And this kind of music could do that.

The waitress brought their drinks.

Noah handed Acacia her whiskey sour. That order had surprised him. He'd expected her to want wine. This was a good choice, though. She'd been on edge all night.

Acacia glanced at him and smiled lazily.

Ah, that was better. It was what this music did. It disarmed you, took away everything but the curling blue edges of the notes sliding so slippery-easy through your head.

He put his arm around her, and she leaned in. A hint of her perfume came to him, and he inhaled. Her scent, light and feminine and a little bit peppery, was unusual but so perfect for her.

The singer ended her number and Acacia set down her drink so she could applaud. "What a fantastic voice. I love this place, Noah," she said softly.

"I was hoping you would." Squeezing her a little closer, he relaxed again as the woman began another song. He felt himself dissolving into the music with each liquid note.

By the end of it, he was in that place, under the blues' magic spell. He cupped Acacia's face and looked into her eyes. Dizzying pleasure spread through him. He kissed her parted lips. So precious. She deserved much more than life had given her. Satiated with the beauty of the music and with the woman in his arms, he turned back to the stage as the next song began.

* * *

Noah pulled up in front of the house and turned off the truck. Acacia still slept, slumped in the seat. The blues did that—relaxed you to the point of sleep when you were already exhausted. Acacia's life wore her out, emotionally as much as physically.

He lifted the console so that he could reach her better and raised her hand to his lips. "Wake up, Sleeping Beauty. We're home."

Her eyes opened, then focused on him. "Hi. I fell asleep?" She sat up, reaching for her purse.

"Yep. Let me get your door."

He held her arm as they walked up the ramp. "Steady there. I don't know how women wear those shoes."

"Honestly, it's not easy. I'm glad I don't do it often." She unlocked the door, and they entered quietly.

Jenny lay sleeping on the couch.

Acacia woke her with a gentle touch on her shoulder.

As Jenny stood, whispering about her evening, Noah paid her.

Acacia thanked the young woman, and they walked her to the door, quietly wishing her a safe trip home.

Noah didn't want the night to end. Not yet. Every nerve in his body was in tune with the woman standing next to him.

Acacia turned, and her look said that maybe she didn't want it to, either.

Something had happened back there at the club, something special. He reached for her and inched her toward him, his gaze never leaving hers.

Close now, she slipped her arms around his neck, and he pulled her to him. She buried her fingers in his hair. If there was one thing that drove Noah crazy, it was having a woman play with his hair. Her nails scraped over his scalp with just the right pressure to send pleasure shooting down his spine. Her dark eyes were wide, searching. He covered her mouth with his in a slow, warm, exploring kiss that quickly went from sweet and tentative to explosive heat. How long had he wanted her? How long had he waited?

She returned his kiss, pressing her body to him, pulling herself up as if begging for more.

He pushed her to the wall, cupping her face in his hands and exploring her with his tongue, stroking her lips, teasing her, feeling her trembling against him. He ran his hand along the length of her body, cupped the curve of a full breast. Even through the layers of her dress and bra, he could feel the firm ball of her nipple. He wanted to pinch it, love on it, but there was too much fabric in the way. He kissed her harder, and she arched into his body.

Breathing fast, he pushed his thigh between her legs, and she whimpered.

He stopped cold.

The sound had been enough to bring him to his senses. What in the hell was he doing? This was Bobby's sister. Was he crazy? Hell, he was taking advantage of a highly vulnerable person. Her first night out in who knew how long and he was on her like a hound dog in heat. Dammit, he was an asshole.

He pushed himself away from the wall—away from her. "I'm so sorry, Acacia. I shouldn't have done that."

"Wh-what?"

"Look, you deserve better than... Well, you've got a lot going on, so much to deal with, and here... Dammit, I just can't, okay?" God, what in the *hell* had he been thinking?

She raised her hand to her lips, her eyes confused. "Noah..."

He moved to the door. "Look, I had a great time tonight. Can we just...?" He blew out a breath. "Acacia, I'll see you in a couple of days, all right?"

Chapter Seven

Acacia stood where he'd left her for a long moment, stunned by what had just happened. What did he mean by saying she had "a lot going on?" He'd known about Bobby from the beginning. Why would he suddenly have cold feet about her responsibilities if he'd always understood them? She bent and stepped out of her shoes. She should have expected this. Who would seriously want to be part of her life? They'd be crazy to take on what she lived with every day. She didn't blame Noah. She'd run for the hills if she were him, too.

As she turned the living room lamp off, a desolation deeper than she could bear settled in her belly. It lay there, black, heavy and unmoving. Funny, she'd thought she would cry, but tears were a million miles away. Closing her eyes, she felt a deep hollowness overwhelm her, bringing with it an oppressive weight. She had nothing—just emptiness. A long, barren road ahead of her for the rest of her life.

Stripping the royal-blue dress off, she left it wadded on the floor. Lying chilled in the bed, feeling the aloneness that would be hers forever, she buried the silly hope that had grown over the past few weeks. *Oh, God, I should have known. Why didn't I see this coming?*

* * *

Two days later, Acacia paced the kitchen. Noah would be here any minute, and she couldn't bear the thought of seeing him. She'd felt she was ready, having spent the last two days preparing herself for his arrival this afternoon. But all that had been for nothing, apparently. Her heart raced, and the tears she hadn't been able to shed before sprang to her eyes. She dabbed at them with a paper towel. No way would she let him see her bawl. She'd fixed her hair, put on makeup, and dressed in jeans and a nice T-shirt. This girl wasn't meeting him at the door looking like a woman who'd been dumped.

The doorbell rang. Her heart pounded fiercely. She bit her lip hard, focusing on the pain. There, that was better. She would not think about Noah. It was all about Bobby today. Throwing her shoulders back, she left the room.

Noah clasped her hand as soon as she opened the door. "Acacia, I need to—"

Yanking her hand from his, she said pleasantly, "Come in. Bobby's ready for you." *Oh God, don't let him touch me again. I can't cry in front of him.*

She walked over to her brother and gave him a hug. "Noah's here. You work hard for him, now." Without looking at Noah, she headed for the back porch and shut the sliding glass door with a solid thump.

Her knees gave out halfway to her seat, and she landed in a heap in the chair. Seeing him was as horrible as she'd thought it would be. She leaned her forehead in her palm. What did he start to say, anyway? Didn't he know that nothing he could say would make things better? Why would he try?

Honestly, from the obvious bags under Noah's eyes, it didn't look like he'd been having a very good time of it, either. Better he get dumping her out of his system now, though, before he left her at the altar. She sighed. Been there, done that, didn't want to do it again.

She picked up her basket and shears and started work in her garden. But peace wouldn't come. Her hands shook. She couldn't concentrate. The third time she missed what she was aiming for and snipped a bloom off her tomato plant, she gave up.

Noah had become such a huge part of their life that to cut him out was like shearing off a limb. Even now, with his voice murmuring in the other room, and despite what she wished, it hurt.

But he was good for Bobby. Her brother needed Noah, and she wouldn't do anything to jeopardize that. Crossing her arms on the table, she laid her head down, closing her eyes. Sleep hadn't crossed her path much since she saw Noah last. Surely this devastation would feel better with time? It had to. She couldn't take much more.

* * *

Noah quietly opened the porch door and stepped outside. Acacia was asleep, her head on her arms. She couldn't be comfortable. Despite her makeup, she looked horribly exhausted today. He must speak with her. Obviously she was very upset with him, but he had to explain why he'd left in such a hurry Tuesday night. She'd trusted him, and he'd abused that trust. He'd taken advantage of her vulnerability, and there was no excuse for it. He prayed she'd forgive him. He didn't know what he'd do if she didn't.

He moved over to the table, then leaned down and gently squeezed her hand. "Acacia? Can we talk?"

She lifted her head, squinting then focusing her eyes on him. "What?" Then she stood so fast she knocked her chair over. "Are you done? I'm sorry. I fell asleep." She turned toward the door.

He placed his hand on her arm to stay her.

She flinched but held still.

"Acacia, will you please let me talk to you?"

She wouldn't look at him. "It's not necessary. I understand where you're coming from just fine." Pulling her arm free, she took a step.

"Please, Acacia."

She stopped.

He turned her toward him. Her beautiful brown eyes stared into his, full of dread. Why, in God's name? Had he hurt her that badly? *Dammit to hell!* Taking a deep breath to regain his composure, he said, "Acacia, I handled everything wrong the other night." She started to speak, but he held up his hand. "Please, let me finish. Bobby's a client. You're his sister. I need to respect that."

Her eyes darkened, and she sucked in her bottom lip.

"And I just moved right in on you, even though I knew you had a lot on your plate."

Her eyes widened, growing even darker.

"I guess what I'm trying to say is that I took advantage. And I shouldn't have."

Tears pooled in her eyes, and she made a strangled sound.

He watched in shock as she rushed into the house and disappeared in the direction of the bedrooms. What in the *hell* had he done now?

He sank into the chair and put his head in his hands. How could he leave her this way? He couldn't walk out the door with her so distraught, but everything he said made it worse. He had to do something.

Having no idea which bedroom was hers, he listened outside each door. Behind the one at the end of the hall, he heard muffled sounds. After listening for a few seconds, he was sure they sounded like crying. He should have his ass kicked. Tapping on the door, he said, "Acacia?"

The sounds stopped.

He tapped louder. "Acacia?"

"Please go away. I'm fine."

"Can I talk to you?"

A sob. "Oh, I think you've said enough."

Dammit, it *was* what he'd said. He had to get in there. "Please, let me in."

"I swear to God, Noah..."

He grinned. Well, she still had some fight in her. "Please?"

"Noah!" After a pause, her voice was just on the other side of the door. "I'm not letting you in. And we will never discuss this again. You're a wonderful therapist for Bobby, and I want you to work with him. Let's please just keep it at that. Now go home."

Stunned, he blinked his eyes. That was it? He couldn't see her anymore? *Hell, no.* They couldn't end this way. He stepped backward and grabbed the wall. How had this happened?

Taking a deep breath, he went into the living room and stopped by Bobby's wheelchair. "See you next week, buddy. You work hard with Bobo and Acacia, okay?" Noah didn't hear

Bobby's answer as he walked out the door. It was over. He and Acacia were done.

Chapter Eight

The next day, Acacia threw a beach towel over her shoulder and headed to the backyard, loaded down with her super-sized insulated cup full of wine, her phone, and her suntan lotion, certain that if she heard one more high-pitched cartoon voice, she would scream.

When the bath aide had called to say she was sick, it had been perfect timing. Acacia couldn't stand the thought of talking to anyone today and had told the woman not to find a replacement. After giving Bobby a quick bed bath, Acacia had fed him breakfast. She'd even skipped his physical therapy exercises without the slightest twinge of guilt.

Her bitchy mood had been obvious when she'd opened her eyes this morning. Her brother didn't deserve to bear the brunt of her ugly state of mind, hence the self-banishment to the backyard.

Spreading out the towel on the lounge chair that she'd set up earlier, she slathered on sunblock. This was her first time lying out this year, and she didn't want to burn. It would be nice to have someone to do her back, but therein lay reason number 9,360 to be the B-word today. She had nobody to rub lotion on her back, and she never would.

She took three long swallows of wine. Part of being a bitch was that you got to break all the rules. It wasn't even noon yet, and she was already hitting the wine—hard. Tough titty. Lying down on her tummy allowed the hot rays of the sun to beat down on her back. Bring it on, sun. She could take its fury and then some.

With her phone blaring, she closed her eyes, hoping the shakes she'd had since she'd seen Noah would subside.

It wasn't working. She turned the volume up. Visions of Noah still bashed her consciousness, despite the hardest rock music she could stand. What would it take to banish him from her mind?

She'd been awake all night, going over every word he'd said, every minute of their date. Not that she'd wanted to. Her brain was relentless. She'd prayed for peace, begged God to make the visions go away. Yet here was the man, still driving her crazy.

She swallowed some more wine, the liquid deliciously cold as it slid down her throat. Damn Noah. Why couldn't he be honest? Why make up those ridiculous excuses? If he thought Bobby was too much, then say so. She'd had her big girl panties on. She could have taken it. It was so dishonest of him to blame other things. And his excuses were so lame.

This drew her back to Johnny and the excuses he'd made to her. He had to run the ranch. She understood, didn't she? He couldn't spend time running back and forth to San Antonio when he had livestock to care for. And everyone knew how long-distance relationships went. They never worked out. Better to end it now, before either of them got hurt.

This was all before they knew the full extent of Bobby's needs. Johnny had broken up with her three weeks before their wedding, when their invitations had been out for months. The guy was a coward. He wasn't man enough to say that he couldn't deal with Bobby and the burden he represented. It had been all about excuses.

And here she was, dealing with excuses again. Yesterday, each reason Noah had given her had driven a stake deeper into her heart. She was a client. She was too weak for a relationship. He'd taken advantage of her. She ground her teeth. It was so ridiculous.

First of all, Bobby was the client, not her. And, Acacia Richards, weak? Give her a freaking break! She'd been through hard times before and come out just fine. And Noah thought he'd taken advantage of her? Oh, that was the *real* winner. Since when had she ever let a man take advantage of her? She gulped some more wine and flipped her head over to the other side. The man was too much of a coward to tell the truth. He didn't want to be a part of her having "a lot on her plate".

The shaking wouldn't stop—like a phone vibrating through her whole body. Her cup was empty, and the wine had gone straight to her head. She'd hoped it would calm her, but it hadn't. She squeezed her eyes tight shut. Things had been bad before, but this? She *missed* Noah, and she hated admitting it. He didn't deserve it. She missed him like hell, and it was killing her.

Turning over on her back, she got comfortable, then raised her hands to her shoulders and softly ran her fingertips down to the ends of her hands. Then she raised her hands and slowly did it again. And again. And again. She rubbed her fingers in slow circles around her belly, around, and around, swirling gently. In time, her shakes went away. One thing had always been true, and she mustn't forget it. She had herself.

* * *

Noah finished topping off the water trough in the steers' pen. It had been a hell of a Monday. Clients had noticed his lack of concentration more than once. It was so unlike him that one client had actually stopped working and asked if he could help Noah. He was all hollow inside. Hungry, but not for food. He was raw and hurting, and nothing made him feel better. The one thing he needed, he couldn't have. Because she wouldn't have him. He turned off the water and wound up the hose.

Back at the house, he pulled a cold beer out of the fridge and sat in the rocker on the porch. The worst part about it all was that she refused to talk to him. She wasn't an unreasonable person. At least, she'd never seemed that way. Had he completely misread her? Hell, he knew she was having a rough time, but this was different.

All he had wanted to do was protect her, to treat her right. Yet, somehow, he'd done everything wrong, and now... He took several swallows of beer and looked off into the pasture. There must be a way. He couldn't give up. He wouldn't. But, for now, he needed to accept her decision. She had that right.

* * *

Bobby lay fast asleep in his bed, yet Acacia was wide awake, images of Noah battering against her skull. No matter how hard she tried, she couldn't get him out of her head, not permanently. Taking a glass of wine, she strode to the dark back porch, lighting a candle on the table beside her chair and forgetting all about checking for snakes. She dialed her cell, hoping her friend could bring some peace to her this night. "Sarah? Kids in bed?"

"Yes, but Colin's fighting it, little stinker. How are you?"

"I'm losing my mind. I can't get thoughts of Noah to leave me alone. What can I do?"

"Oh, sweetie. I know it's hard. At some point, though, you've got to let someone in."

"It's not that. He's made it clear he doesn't want my problems. He practically ran away from me."

"I don't understand what happened that night. Why not ask him? Let him tell you in plain words what he was feeling. He seems to be a great guy."

Acacia sighed. "He seems that way, all right. But I think the message was real clear. The man doesn't want what my life entails."

"I just feel like you need to talk to him. What could it hurt?"

Acacia gritted her teeth. What could it hurt? Memories of Johnny's betrayal flooded her. It could hurt quite a lot, actually. "I think it's obvious where we stand." She bit her lip. "I'm wondering about something, though. Should I request a different therapist? It's painful seeing him. Every minute he's in this house it hurts. But he's so perfect for Bobby, and Bobby adores him. I don't know what to do."

"Oh, no. Don't change. Don't take him away from Bobby. Acacia, you can work this out. Give it some time, okay? You'll find a way."

She didn't argue, but inside, not a trickle of hope remained.

* * *

Tuesday afternoon, Noah waited for Acacia to answer the door, his heart racing. How would she react? By some miracle, would things be back to normal? The lock clicked, and he forced a smile. "Hi." His heart plummeted. The look on her face said that things were definitely not back to normal.

She stepped back. "Come in. Bobby's ready for you."

Disappointment weighed down his boots. What could he do to change her mind? He couldn't bear for this to go on. Somehow, he had to make her understand. If only there were some way to get her to listen. Her cold, closed expression gave him little hope, though. The last thing she appeared to want was to talk to him.

Bobby grinned at Noah as he walked over. "I'm having a party. Come to my birthday, Noah?"

Acacia, who had been walking out of the room, stopped mid-stride.

Noah waited, unsure of how to respond. Would she want him to come?

Acacia turned, her face blank. "Noah, we'd be happy to have you attend. It's this coming Saturday. Our parents will be here, and so will my friend Sarah and her family. Oh, and Jenny."

Noah nodded to Bobby. "I'd love to come, buddy. What do you want for your birthday?"

Bobby laughed. "Presents!"

"I'll bring one, then." Before Acacia could leave, he asked, "What time?"

"Three o'clock, here at the house." She gave him a lopsided, uneasy smile. "And a present really isn't necessary."

"I'll be here, and with a present."

She walked to the sliding doors and went outside.

He wished he could reach her somehow, break through the barrier she held between them.

Noah started the movement and stretching exercises on Bobby's arms, his mind focused on the woman who sat a short distance away. But it might as well be a thousand miles. How could he change this mess? He had to give her time. How much time, though? Acacia was worn down and upset. He couldn't push her. But he wouldn't let it go, either. She meant too much to him. And he'd meant something to her, too. He was sure of it. That feeling for him had to be in there somewhere. Hopefully, underneath it all, she still cared for him.

Taking out the ball on a string, he asked, "You ready for some baseball?"

Bobby laughed. "Yeah."

Soon, it was time for lower body exercises. Using the lift, he lowered Bobby to the blanket on the floor.

Acacia walked in with her empty tea glass. "How's it going, brother?"

"I played base-ball."

She smiled at them and headed into the kitchen.

Noah's chest tightened. God, it was great to see that smile, even if it included her brother. He'd missed her smiles; missed working together with her on Bobby's therapy. It was so hard coming here and not being with her. He'd even considered suggesting that another therapist take over when it appeared that things would continue this way, but he couldn't do that to Bobby, and he couldn't give up on Acacia. She was worth waiting for.

He lifted Bobby's leg, stretching the muscles and ligaments, holding the position while he counted in his head. Having Acacia beside him at the jazz club had been...well, he couldn't describe it. But she'd entered his world, the one the blues created for him, and no one had ever done that before. That night had been the best high he'd ever had.

Acacia walked back out to the porch, her eyes straight ahead.

Ahh. She didn't want to look at him. Heaving a deep sigh, he set the leg down, raising Bobby's other leg and holding it in place. To have their evening together end in the way it did—he'd never seen it coming. He should have. He should have taken better care of her. He should have realized how vulnerable she was. If he could only go back in time...

But he couldn't do that. Weight settled on his shoulders as he worked on Bobby's hip flexibility, then his knees. In time, Bobby's exercises were done, and Noah helped him back into his wheelchair and set him up in front of his cartoons.

He couldn't leave. He needed more. He walked to the back and opened the sliding door. "We're finished."

She looked up and smiled, then dropped it. "Okay. I'll get him some juice and a snack."

He stood in the door for a moment as she approached, taking in the small details of her appearance. She looked so damned worn out. "How are you, Acacia?"

"Fine. Just fine." She stopped a few feet from him.

Her shuttered face gave him nothing. He wanted to grab her, hold her, kiss her—anything to break through to this zombie-like woman. But he couldn't do that. When it seemed that she wouldn't say anymore, he backed up, returning to the living room.

Squeezing Bobby's shoulder, he walked out the door. He had to give her time, but it sure was hard as hell to do.

* * *

Saturday afternoon, holding the promised gift and a bouquet of flowers, Noah rang the doorbell. Judging by the number of cars in front of the house, he must be the last to arrive at the birthday party. The door opened, and he clutched the presents tighter.

Acacia smiled at him, then jerked her gaze away.

He sucked in a breath. *Look at me! See me. Don't you know how much I care for you? Can't you see it in my eyes?* It was no use.

He cleared his throat nervously. "Looks like everybody's here but me."

She stepped back, still avoiding his eyes. "We haven't started yet. You're not late."

He offered her the bouquet. "These are for you. After all, it's your birthday too."

She met his gaze, and he saw the pain in her eyes before she looked down at the blooms. "Thank you, Noah. They're beautiful." She took the vase from him.

Bobby yelled, "Noah! Noah's here," when he walked into the living room.

George and Rebecca sat on the couch. He went over and shook hands with them. "Good to see you again."

Rebecca smiled warmly. "I'm so glad you're here."

"I wouldn't miss it."

"Grab a chair. Take a load off." George motioned to the recliner in the corner.

Acacia had followed Noah. "I can take the gift. We've set up a table for them."

Their fingers brushed as she took the bag. Little tingles raced up his arm. God, he'd missed her.

She'd gone all out on the decorations. Colorful streamers crisscrossed the ceiling and balloons hung from them in strategic places. A birthday banner spanned the archway into the kitchen where colored plates, cups, and flatware sat on a bright tablecloth on the dining table. The cake was one of Bobby's favorite cartoon characters.

Bobby nodded his head for attention. "Noah, I got a hat. It's my birth-birthday hat."

"Hey, you look cool, buddy."

"Help me blow." Bobby looked down in his lap and moved his arm in jerky circles.

Noah spied his kazoo and picked up the small cylinder, placing it between his lips.

Bobby blew with all his might, and a loud noise split the air. Noah released it and Bobby threw his head back, laughing. "I blow good."

Noah grinned. "Uh, yes, you do. That was really loud." Something touched his elbow, and he turned.

Acacia stood with an attractive blonde of about the same age. Without meeting Noah's gaze, she said, "Noah, this is my best friend, Sarah."

He reached out his hand. "Hi. Nice to meet you."

Sarah grinned and shook his hand. "Great to meet you too, cowboy. I've heard lots about you."

A dark pink flush rose up Acacia's neck.

So she'd talked about him to her best friend. Nice. He asked Sarah, "Are you from North Texas?"

"Born and raised in Howelton, just like my bestie here. My better half's in the kitchen. I left him watching the stove. I've got two kids in the backyard, too." She ran her gaze up and down Noah. "So, let's hear more about you."

Acacia rolled her eyes and went back into the kitchen.

Noah's gaze followed her, noting what must be a new pair of jeans. These were formfitting, outlining her sexy behind in a way her old ones hadn't. A sheer white shirt let the simple chemise she wore underneath peek through. He pressed his lips together. He wanted this woman. What in the *hell* could he do to make her his?

"Do you have any brothers or sisters, Noah?"

He flicked his gaze back to Sarah. "Yeah, I do. I have an older brother, Joe, and a little sister."

"Noah, I need help," Bobby called.

Thank God. The last thing he wanted to do was talk about his brother. "Okay, buddy. Excuse me." He nodded to Sarah as he headed over to Bobby and knelt in front of him. "What do you need?"

"I want to open my presents."

Noah grinned. "I'll bet you do. Let me ask your sister what's going on."

Bobby sighed heavily. "Okay."

He found Acacia still in the kitchen, along with a man who must be Sarah's husband. "Acacia? Bobby's getting impatient to open his presents."

The corner of her mouth lifted and she shook her head. "Again? It must be the tenth time he's asked today. I'm hoping to wait until after we eat." She glanced at Noah and then at the other man. "Oh, Tom? This is Noah, Bobby's physical therapist. Noah, this is Sarah's husband, Tom."

Noah grasped the man's hand. "Nice to meet you. How was the drive from Howelton?"

"The drive was fine. Getting my three up early and on the road was the chore. They're all sleepyheads."

"Well, I'm glad you made it."

Noah turned back to Acacia. Such a kissable mouth. It beckoned to him. He loved that she wore red lipstick. So many women couldn't carry it off, but red looked like it was made for her full lips.

"Noah? Would you like a beer?" Tom asked.

"Sure."

Tom grabbed two out of the ice chest. "Why don't we step outside? I need to check on my kids. They're being way too quiet."

As Noah walked away, his connection to Acacia faded, and a heaviness settled on his chest. He glanced back from the doorway. Acacia's gaze had followed him. He glimpsed some of his own pain on her face.

She blinked, and that look was gone.

What did it mean? Was she hurting, too? If so, wasn't that a good sign? An indication that she still cared for him?

Tom called to his children as he opened the sliding doors.

Noah followed him outside, Acacia filling his thoughts.

After dinner, Bobby finally got to open his presents. Colin, Sarah's oldest, and Cara, her six-year-old, helped him. Colin knew how to play it. He yanked each present out with a big *Ta-da!*, which made Bobby howl with laughter. Noah's gift of small brass cymbals that attached to Bobby's wrists with Velcro straps was the biggest hit of the afternoon.

After Bobby had clapped them together a couple of times with Noah's help, Acacia laughed. "Thanks heaps."

Noah asked innocently, "What? This is good for his therapy goal." He figured her laughter was another good sign.

Acacia shook her head, not meeting his eyes, but still grinning.

While Acacia and Rebecca were dishing up cake and ice cream, Sarah pulled Noah aside. "Can we go outside for a minute?"

Noah drew his brows together. "Sure. What's up?"

Without answering, she motioned for him to follow her.

Out on the back porch, she stood in the far corner, away from view of those in the house. "You can probably see that Acacia's been under tremendous stress."

"Yeah, I've noticed. Is something wrong? I've asked, but she says she's fine."

Sarah groaned. "That girl! She's *not* fine. Her mammogram came back abnormal. She has an ultrasound scheduled this coming week, and she's worried sick, what with her mom having breast cancer and all. She hasn't been sleeping, either. I know I shouldn't be telling you this, but she needs somebody here in San Antonio who cares about her to know. And I'm sure you care."

What the hell? And Acacia hadn't told him? This was serious! "Yes, I do care. I care a lot. I wish she would let me in. But she's shut me out."

"I'm sorry, Noah. It's complicated. Just hang in there, okay? Don't give up on her."

He pressed his lips together. "I don't plan on it. Thanks for telling me. I'll do what I can. Whatever she'll let me do."

Acacia frowned at them when they walked back into the kitchen. "Where did you two get off to?"

Sarah answered with a question. "What does a girl have to do to get some cake and ice cream around here?"

Acacia handed her a plate, still frowning.

Noah put out his hand. "Me, too, please."

Shaking her head, she gave him a plate. "I know you two were plotting something. I'll find out what it is. I have Sarah's number after all these years, believe you me."

Sarah giggled. "She does. I can't hide a thing from her."

An hour later, as Sarah and Tom were preparing to leave, Noah pulled Acacia aside. "Sarah told me about the ultrasound you have coming up. Please let me know if you need anything. I'm here for you. I hope you know that."

Acacia sighed and shook her head. "Sarah. That girl. Thank you, Noah. I appreciate the offer, but I'll be fine."

He blew out a frustrated breath. "I mean it, Acacia. I want to help."

Driving home, possible ramifications of the abnormal mammogram ran through Noah's mind, the worst being breast cancer. She must let him in. She had nobody here. Her parents had the ranch to run. They couldn't be away for long—and her mother had breast cancer herself. Sarah worked and had two young children. Plus, she was in Howelton. How much help could she be? Something had to change. He gripped the steering wheel. God had to answer his prayers. Acacia needed him.

Chapter Nine

Acacia shifted in her seat at the doctor's office. Beige décor and a sterile setting did nothing to improve her anxious mood. The one corn plant in the corner hardly spruced up the place. How come she'd never noticed how depressing this room was before?

The VA caregiver was with Bobby today, so this appointment had to run on time. The woman had to leave at four-thirty. Acacia checked her watch again. What was taking so long? She'd already been waiting forty-five minutes. If the look on the ultrasound tech's face last week meant anything, she wouldn't be getting good news. Of course, the tech hadn't been able to tell her anything, and not knowing had been hell. She couldn't fall asleep once she got to bed, and even when she did get to sleep, she woke up at least two or three times during the night, worrying about the outcome of this meeting with her doctor.

The toll on her mother as she'd fought her cancer had been terrible. First the surgery, then radiation, and now the chemotherapy had sapped her strength completely. Her mom was a walking ghost of her former self, yet she'd had Acacia's father to care for her through the whole process.

Acacia squeezed her eyes shut. How could she take care of Bobby and go through cancer treatments too? What would happen to him if she fell apart?

She imagined driving herself home, sick to death from a chemo treatment, and tears pooled behind her eyelids. *Please, God, don't let this be cancer. Please let the lump be benign.*

Someone called her name. She opened her eyes to see one of the nurses standing by the open door, smiling.

Her heart sped up. In a few moments, she'd have an answer. Suddenly, she wished Noah was with her, that he had his warm, strong arm around her as she walked toward her fate. A shudder passed through her. But she couldn't give in to fear. Her mother had faced cancer with courage. She would too.

Her doctor waited for her in his office. He stood and shook her hand. "Sit down, Acacia. Let's talk about your ultrasound results, shall we?"

"Yes. Thank you." Despite her efforts, fear coiled in her belly, freezing her face muscles, making it an effort to smile.

He opened a folder on his desk, then met her gaze. "I'm afraid they're not what we'd hoped for, but they could be much worse, too. The results show a tumor that appears to be problematic. Your lump has irregular edges, and the heat signature points to a possibility of cancer. Of course, we won't be sure until it can be biopsied."

She blinked. "Problematic? Cancer?"

"Possibly. But, please don't worry at this point. We need to have a look at the tumor and take a tissue sample. I'll recommend a surgeon, though you're free to choose someone else if you have another doctor in mind. It's important that we jump on this right away, though. We shouldn't wait to deal with it."

Her brain had frozen at the word *cancer*. Nothing made sense. A surgeon? What for? What was happening? "I'm sorry. What are you recommending?"

He took off his glasses and laid them on the desk. "Your surgeon can give you more details, as can your oncologist. I can recommend an oncologist, and I'm sure your surgeon can refer you to some as well. In general, the first step in your treatment is to remove the tumor, and maybe a few lymph nodes, too, to see if any are involved. Everything will be biopsied. These biopsies will determine your further treatment. After surgery, if cancer is present, you'll need radiation therapy and, depending on the amount of lymph node involvement, you may also receive chemotherapy."

Numbness spread through her body, seeping into her mind. Radiation? Chemotherapy? Those treatments had torn her mother to shreds. She tried to speak, but her mouth wouldn't move. Slowly, her tongue wet her lips. "So, I...what? I call this surgeon now?"

"My staff will be glad to make the appointment for you. Stop by the desk on the way out, and they'll work with you on that. But, remember, let's do this right away, okay?"

She nodded, still in a daze. *I might have cancer.* She stood and headed for the door. *Cancer. I might have cancer.* They say breast cancer is hereditary, but she'd always thought it would happen to someone else. She ground her teeth. Not with her luck. Her life didn't work like that.

After making the appointment, she headed to the van in a fog, drove home on autopilot, and didn't remember telling Bobby's caregiver goodbye. Out on the porch, she curled into her chair, covering her head with her arms. Numb. Empty. Alone. Where would the courage she needed to face cancer come from? A vision of Noah came to her again. God, why couldn't things be different? Settling into his arms that night at the club had been so perfect. His strength had poured into her. If only she had that now.

She hated herself for thinking it, but what would her life be like without her brother? Would a man like Noah accept her, love her, want her for his wife? Would things be easy, happy, from the beginning for her? Her relationship had been that way with Johnny at first. Not perfect, but it had been good. She hadn't worried that he'd leave her back then.

Bobby was a permanent game changer. Part of her life forever. And she wouldn't change that. No way would she dump him, put him somewhere without his family. He didn't deserve that. She wouldn't do it.

She sucked in a breath. She must face this. Now. There was no time to feel sorry for herself. Her lips quivered. It was no use. *I might have cancer. I might have cancer.* The trembling started in the middle of her chest—a vibration that quickly moved to her arms, hands, and legs. She could die without ever having married. Without ever giving birth to the babies she'd dreamed of. She might be dead come this time next year.

She squeezed her arms tighter. Tears leaked from her eyes. Her parents couldn't deal with Bobby. They'd try, and the effort would ruin them. They'd have to put him in a home. Her brother would be destroyed. A sob escaped her. *I might have cancer, and I could die.* Still trembling, she tried to imagine dying. She couldn't, though. Not today.

She raised her head and rubbed away her tears, softly stroking her hands down her face, over and over, soothing herself. Then she stroked her arms, tenderly, gently, as calm returned to her. She always, always had herself. Maybe she would die. But maybe she wouldn't. She'd live life one day at a time. Find her strength one day at a time. It might not be courage, but at least she could do that.

After supper, she gave Bobby his cymbals and put his *Kids Bop* music on before she went outside to call her mom. She'd dreaded calling them all afternoon. Not wanting her parents to worry, she hadn't told them about her abnormal mammogram. This would be a shock for them. She dialed and waited. The phone clicked. It was her mom. "Hi, Mom. Is Dad there with you?"

"He's not in yet, honey. He's checking the pastures right now. Do you need him to call you?"

She'd hoped her dad would be there to support her mom. "No, that's not necessary. Mom, something's come up. I need to talk to you." With as few details as possible, she told her mom about her upcoming appointment with the surgeon and the treatments she might undergo.

"Honey, no," her mom cried. "Not you too." She sobbed into the phone.

This was as horrible as Acacia had imagined it would be. Her poor mom had so much on her plate already, and now this? The situation was so unfair. "Mom, if it *is* cancer, we caught this early. I'll be fine, okay? Please don't cry."

Her mom sniffed and gulped loudly. "Oh, honey, I'm sorry. I need to be strong for you, and here I am blubbering in your ear. Of course you'll be all right. Listen, your dad and I will come up the day before the surgery. One of us will go with you to the hospital, and the other will stay with Bobby. You don't worry about a thing. We'll stay for a few days until you're back on your feet. Dad can ask Uncle Dan to look after things around here, like he always does."

"Oh, Mom. What would I do without you guys? You're such an example to me. I'll make it through this."

After she hung up, she had one more call to make. She dialed Sarah's number.

She answered, "Tell me quick. What did you find out?"

Acacia gave her the details, leaving out nothing, knowing it would save a million questions.

When she'd finished, Sarah said quietly, "I'm glad your parents are coming, but there's someone else who will want to be there. Noah cares about you. You need to tell him as soon as you find out when this is happening. Promise me you will."

Acacia was silent.

"Promise me?"

"I don't think so."

"Acacia, the man should know. Promise you'll at least think about it?"

Acacia sighed. Sarah could be so dang pushy. "Okay, I'll think about it."

"Of course you'll tell me the second you hear anything."

Acacia laughed. "You'll be the first."

* * *

Noah drew in a sharp breath when Acacia opened the door. The woman looked terrible.

She stepped aside and let him in the door.

Dark circles under her eyes cut deep into her face. Broken capillaries colored the whites of her eyes pink. What the *hell* was going on?

"Your favorite person is here, Bobby," she called out as they walked inside.

He had to find out what was happening. Acacia couldn't keep pushing him away. Her appearance made it obvious—she needed help. Was it about the ultrasound? How could he find out? Why hadn't he asked for Sarah's number when he had the chance?

He set his bag in front of Bobby, who was grinning at him. "Hey there, buddy. You ready to work?"

"Yeah, Noah. I'm ready."

"Good."

Acacia walked out to the back, as usual.

He started with something fun. "How about some music today?"

While he worked Bobby's upper body, he tried to figure out how to approach Acacia. If he straight-up asked her what was wrong, he doubted she'd admit to anything. Yet there must be a way to find out. The last thing he did with Bobby was baseball, which he enjoyed, as always.

He raised Bobby with the lift and laid him on the floor for his lower body exercises. In the twenty minutes it took to complete those, he'd come up with a plan.

After settling Bobby back in front of his cartoons, he headed for the sliding glass doors, his pulse racing. This was like facing a she-bear in her den. He stepped outside and settled himself in one of the porch chairs.

Acacia's eyes opened wide. She obviously hadn't expected that.

"Bobby did great on his therapy, as usual. I wish all my patients worked as hard." He looked for a response.

Her eyes narrowed, and she waited for him to go on.

Damn. The woman wasn't going to make this easy.

She finally nodded. "He always was one to work hard."

That was all she had? He sighed. "What's happening on the medical front?" The question didn't leave her room for a *just fine* answer.

Clenching her hands together, she looked down as she answered. "My ultrasound results weren't good. My tumor is 'problematic'. I'm meeting with a surgeon to plan the surgery."

The blood drained from his face, leaving him lightheaded. Acacia? Surgeon? She was having surgery! "Tell me when it is—"

She cut in. "There's really no point, is there?"

He gritted his teeth. God, she was driving him crazy. "Just let me know, okay? I'm here to help. Always."

Looking away, she hesitated for a few seconds, then nodded.

* * *

A week later, Acacia cuddled the phone on her shoulder and looked off into the night. She needed to hear Sarah's voice. Sipping wine, she listened to her friend talk about the little things in her life. Sarah had always known how to soothe her. After talking for thirty minutes, Acacia felt better than she had in days.

Sarah broke into her thoughts. "So, how's Noah?"

Noah? Now there was a topic she didn't want to explore. "Fine, I guess. I don't stick around while he works with Bobby."

"He knows about the surgery, right?"

"Sort of."

Sarah huffed. "How can someone sort of know about a surgery?"

"He knows I'm going to have surgery, but not exactly when."

Sarah was silent for a moment.

"At least I told him I had an appointment with a surgeon."

"Why don't you cut the guy some slack? Call him up and tell him when your surgery is."

Acacia sighed. She really didn't want to do that. "It'll only make things worse. I'm trying so hard to get him out of my head, but I can't. I dream about him, I think about him all the time. I miss him, and I don't want to. Sarah, it hurts so much that I won't have a husband, or babies, or the life I always dreamed of. With Noah, I glimpsed it again. I let myself hope. Now it hurts ten times worse to let it go. The pain is tearing me up inside. I don't *want* to talk to him. Can you understand that?"

"Baby, I hear what you're saying, but I have a gut feeling about Noah. Give him a chance, and I think you'll see he's different. I don't quite know how it'll all work out, but I believe it will."

Acacia sighed. "Sarah, Sarah. I do love you."

"I love you too. Now you have four days before your surgery. That gives you plenty of time to get your courage up for that phone call."

* * *

Wednesday evening, the phone rang just as Acacia and Bobby were finishing supper. "Hi, Mom. What's up?"

"Honey, we're in a real mess here. And I can't make your father listen to reason. He passed out today while he was on the tractor. Ran it into some mesquite trees. He's not sure how long he was unconscious. Of course, he won't go get checked. Says it was the heat, but that tractor is air-conditioned. He still wants to drive down there tomorrow but, honey, I'm scared. What if it happens again?"

"Mom, you put him on the phone. I'll talk some sense into him." Her dad was damn sure a stubborn man. Once he made up his mind, it took dynamite to change it.

Her dad picked up the phone. "Hi, sweetheart. How are you?"

"We're not talking about me, mister. We're talking about you and how you won't go get checked at the doctor's tomorrow. I absolutely won't let you come down here until you've done that. I've got this whole hospital thing covered. If you come down here without finding out what's wrong with you, I'll be so worried I won't recover from my surgery. Then how will you feel?"

"Dammit, honey. I'm fine. I just got too hot."

"Bullshit, Dad. The tractor's got AC. Something happened to you, and you have to find out what it was. Period. Got it? Don't make Mom worry any more about this. As weak as she is, she can't take it. Promise me you'll go tomorrow?"

"You fight dirty."

"Learned it from my old man."

He grunted. "Okay. I'll go to the doc. But then we're coming down."

Acacia hung up, the panic she'd been holding in check flooding her system. Her surgery was the day after tomorrow.

What the hell would she do now? Wiping Bobby's face, she steered him into the living room and gave him a toy, turning on his favorite show. Didn't Jenny attend classes on Friday? Oh, God. Maybe the VA caregiver could come for an extra day for more hours. She didn't know what the rules were about that. Was it too late to find out? To schedule her?

She poured a glass of wine and grabbed her phone, heading out to the back porch. Pulling in a deep breath, she eased it out. *One thing at a time, Acacia. Panic never helped solve a problem.* She dialed Jenny.

"Hi, Acacia. How are you?"

Her spirits lifted just hearing the young woman's perky voice. "I'm about to lose my mind right now. You remember my surgery's Friday? My mom just called. Dad's sick, and they can't come down. Is there any way you can stay with Bobby?"

"I'm so sorry about your dad, Acacia. Well, let's see. A friend of mine is taking my Friday class, too, so I'll ask her to take notes for me. Sure, I can do it. I'd be glad to."

She let out the breath she'd been holding. "Oh, Jenny. That's so sweet of you. I hate that you're missing class, but I don't know what else to do. I need to leave pretty early, though. Can you be here at 5:45 in the morning? I have to be at the hospital at 6:30. Since I'm having day surgery, I'll be home in the afternoon."

"No problem, Acacia."

After hanging up, she took a sip of wine. One problem solved, one huge one to go. She couldn't very well drive herself home from the hospital. Not after being under general anesthesia. And she didn't trust using something like Uber or a taxi after her surgery. Her options for help were limited, and she didn't like where this was taking her. Picking up her shears, she trimmed some yellow leaves on her tomato plants that the heat had shriveled.

How could she ask? But what choice did she have? She plopped down in her chair and put her face in her hands. Why in the hell did life need to be so hard? Couldn't she keep a shred of dignity? She sighed. It didn't appear so. She had to call him.

She grabbed her phone and dialed before she lost her courage. When Noah answered, she said, "Remember that offer you made?"

"Of course I do. How can I help?"

"My surgery is scheduled on Friday."

"I see."

She should have called him like Sarah had suggested. *Damn.* "My parents were supposed to be here to take care of things, but Dad's not well. Jenny's staying with Bobby, and I was wondering... Would you take me to the hospital and bring me home?" *Crap.* She hated this.

"Sure I will. What's going on with George? Is he okay?"

She told him what had happened. "He's being stubborn, and I'm worried about him. He's always been so strong, but with first Bobby and now caring for Mom during her cancer treatments, I think it's all been too much for him."

"If I can help them in any way, I will. Now tell me, what time do I need to pick you up?"

After telling him the time, she said, "I'm sorry you have to take me so early. I can call you when I'm ready to go home, and you can come pick me up."

He huffed. "Like I'm leaving. I'll wait while you're in surgery, Acacia. And I'll be there after recovery, if you'll let me. You shouldn't be alone for any of this."

God, it sounded wonderful. It wasn't right to want him there, but she did. Having his strength beside her when she faced surgery that day would give her the courage she hoped for. "Thank you, Noah. I appreciate it. I'm sorry I gave you such last-minute notice."

"I told you I'd help in any way I could, and I meant it. I'm here for you. Please try not to worry. I've got you Friday."

When she hung up, she leaned back in her chair and sipped her wine, tension slipping away from her. Noah would be with her. She was safe.

Chapter Ten

Friday morning, while Acacia went to get the small bag she'd packed, Noah pulled Jenny aside. "How long are you scheduled to stay today?"

"I think I'm supposed to leave once she gets back from the hospital, sometime in the afternoon."

Ah, Acacia. He should have known. "Do you mind staying a couple of hours longer? I'll spend the night here. One way or another, I'll talk Acacia into it. She'll be in no shape to care for Bobby after her surgery. But I need to go home and feed and pack a bag."

"Not a problem. I'd be glad to."

Noah hugged her. "Thanks, honey. Give my sister a hug from me, too, when you see her."

Acacia walked back into the living room. "I'm ready, I guess."

Reaching for the bag she carried, he said, "Let's hit the road, then." Her drawn, anxious face worried him.

Acacia gave Jenny a hug. "Thanks again for bailing me out."

Once in the truck, Noah kept up light conversation, hoping to calm Acacia's nerves. Her hands were in constant motion, and she couldn't sit still. He finally reached over and grasped her shoulder, squeezing gently. "Acacia, I'll be there with you today, every step of the way, if you'll let me. I've been praying hard since you told me about your surgery. You'll be fine. Lean on me. I've got your back, okay?"

She stared at him, her eyes round. Taking a deep breath, she nodded. "Okay... Okay. Thanks, Noah."

God, she was scared. He'd give anything to be able to take her in his arms and make it all go away. But she wouldn't like that. She'd come this far, though. She'd allowed him to be here with her. He'd make the best of it.

When they arrived at the hospital, there was the usual paperwork, which Acacia dealt with calmly enough. Then they sat in a waiting room for twenty minutes until a nurse came and called her back to pre-op.

She rose hesitantly. "Just me?"

Surprised, he realized she wanted him with her after all.

"Your husband can come back too. It's okay."

She flipped her head toward him, mouth ajar.

He grinned. "Hubby's coming."

Narrowing her eyes at him, she turned back to the nurse. "Okay, thanks."

They followed the nurse through several corridors until they came to a room separated into eight sections by curtains, some drawn, some not. A few other patients lay on gurneys awaiting their own surgeries.

The nurse led them to an empty cubicle and pulled the curtains closed around them. She pointed to the gown on the gurney. "Take your clothes off, please, and put that on. Your personal articles go in the bag, and your husband can keep them while you're in surgery."

He grinned again. He loved this whole hubby thing.

Acacia scowled at him.

The nurse left, and he said, "Yell when you're ready," and stepped outside the curtains. He had to work hard to keep himself from imagining what was going on behind the thin barrier between them.

In a few minutes, Acacia called, "Okay, come on back in."

She was sitting up on the bed, a sheet covering her legs and hips, looking completely lost.

As he stood by the bed, he made a decision. He would care for her the way he wanted to—the way he felt she needed. If she didn't like it, she'd have to tell him. He picked up her hand and laced his fingers through hers. "Did I tell you Ronnie's been looking at another roping horse?" He'd startled her by taking her hand, but she hadn't pulled away.

She shook her head.

"Yep. His horse is getting a little age on him. He's had him for years. The one he's looking at is only four, and he's good. A rider like Ronnie can make him great."

She breathed a little easier. "What'll he do with the one he has?"

"A high school kid's looking at him. He'll be a perfect horse for him. One like that could teach the kid a lot."

She looked better already. He squeezed her hand. "There you go. Easy now. You're going to be okay."

One side of her mouth twitched up, and she squeezed back. "Thank you for being here with me, Noah."

"You bet. Now tell me, do you like to ride?"

"I do. Just don't get to anymore, now that I live down here."

"Maybe we can do something about that when this is all over."

She turned away, pressing her lips together.

Oh, so we aren't there yet, huh? He wouldn't give up, though. "Bobby's sure got his heart set on getting a mini horse—talks about them all the time. He remembers I said a mini was only as tall as his wheelchair. We need to take him to see some."

She grinned. "He's totally hyped about them. He's seen some minis on TV, and he told me he wants one, too. I do need to take him to see some. I'll bet I could find someplace on the internet. I hadn't thought of that. Thanks for the suggestion, Noah."

Oh, he got *that*, all right. *She'd* take Bobby. Damn, she was tough.

A different nurse came in, and Acacia's eyes grew big again. He squeezed her hand. "Easy there."

The nurse said, "I'm Rose, and I'll be in the OR with you. I'll start your IV now, and your anesthesiologist will be in here in a few minutes."

While the nurse worked, Acacia clutched Noah's fingers hard, keeping her gaze fixed on him.

He smiled into her eyes, sending her strength and reassurance. When the nurse left, Acacia began to fidget again. He tucked a strand of hair behind her ear. "Now, come on. It's fine." Turning her face toward him, he looked into her eyes again. "I'm here with you. It's okay." He stroked her cheek, cupping her face in his palm.

She smiled faintly and sighed.

"I'll be in the waiting room while you're in surgery. They'll call me when you come out of recovery, and I'll come back in here, okay? You won't be alone."

"I just..." She shook her head. "I agreed that if my breast looks worse than they expect, they can take it all. I mean, I'll have a mastectomy." She turned to him, searching his eyes.

"A wise choice. I'm glad you made it, Acacia. With one breast or two, you'll still be beautiful. Surely you know that."

Her bottom lip quivered, and she turned her head.

Swiftly, he pulled her into a hug, holding her tight. "You're beautiful. I've thought it since I first laid eyes on you. Nothing can change that. Now, quit worrying." He drew back and kissed her forehead, then handed her a Kleenex from a nearby dispenser.

A few minutes later, her anesthesiologist came in and checked her IV, then explained her anesthesia.

She clutched Noah's hand like a lifeline. With gentle pressure on her fingers, he let her know she wasn't alone.

Fifteen minutes later, her surgeon came in and shook their hands. Acacia introduced Noah. The surgeon described the procedure he would perform and asked if she had any questions.

Acacia's pale face was tight with worry. "No, I understand."

The surgeon patted her arm. "Okay. We'll get you back there in a few minutes, then."

Noah talked about whatever entered his mind for the next quarter of an hour.

Finally, Rose and an orderly came and pulled open the curtains. The nurse smiled brightly and said, "Time to go." She laid a clipboard at the foot of Acacia's bed as the orderly put up the rails.

Noah pressed Acacia's hand to his lips and kissed her fingers, looking into her eyes. "Don't worry. I'll be here. You're safe."

Her eyes were wide, frightened. She gripped his hand. "Thank you. I'll see you when it's over."

"Yes, you will, honey. I promise." A wave of fear hit him as the gurney rolled away.

* * *

Acacia's hold on her courage slid sideways as Noah's fingers slipped from hers. This was it. She was going in. *Will I wake up with one breast or two? Oh, God!* Taking a deep breath, she concentrated on the ceiling whizzing past. The elastic on the cap she wore pinched around her ear. Why hadn't she noticed that? She reached up and adjusted it.

The orderly said, "We'll be there in a minute. Hang tight."

Hang tight? When I might wake up one breast short? Hang tight, my ass. She gritted her teeth and breathed through her nose. *Easy. Easy, Acacia.* She had a talented surgeon, and a chance of coming out of today with just a lumpectomy. Biting her lip hard, she looked at the nurse at her feet, focusing on her and on the sound of the wheels rolling down the corridor.

She'd been fine as long as Noah was beside her. His hand had been like warm steel, sending strength and peace to her anxious mind. Without him, her fear was seeping back in. *God, if my lump isn't benign, please let the surgeon get all the cancer. I have to be here for Bobby. Surely, God, You won't leave my poor brother alone? I know You won't do that to him.* She squeezed her eyes shut and willed it to be so.

The gurney slowed, and she lifted her head a little. They stopped outside an open door for a few seconds.

Her surgeon walked inside the room.

The orderly pushed her on in, parking her beside a table under hanging lights. Then he helped her shift to the operating surface.

I want Noah! God, how she'd missed him these past weeks. Having him here today had brought it all back. How much she cared for him. How wonderful he was. What had she done, letting him get this close again? Hell, she didn't care. She needed him now.

The room was freezing. Trays of shiny instruments stood ready. Everything else was draped and sterile. Rose bustled about. Acacia's surgeon spoke quietly in the background.

Her anesthesiologist waited beside her. "You doing okay, Acacia?"

She shook her head.

"No? Here, I'll give you a little something. You'll feel much better." Injecting fluid into her IV port, he said, "Now, count backward from one hundred for me."

Oh, Noah! "One hundred, ninety-nine, ninety-eight, ninety-seven, ninety-six..."

* * *

Noah stood again and paced the length of the waiting room. Would they remember to call his name? He'd given it to Rose, but had Acacia put it on her paperwork? He'd forgotten to ask her. Rubbing his jaw, he kept walking. How long had it been? He checked his watch. Only twenty minutes. They'd said an hour and a half. It could go faster, couldn't it? If everything looked good? But what if it didn't? What if it was worse? He clenched his teeth. No, he wouldn't think of that. It'd be good news. His prayers would be answered.

He should call Rebecca and George. Stepping outside into the parking lot, he dialed the number Acacia had given him.

Her mom answered on the first ring.

"Hi, Rebecca. Noah here."

"Thanks so much for calling. Any news?"

He brought her up to speed, then said, "They'll come and get me when she's out of recovery. I went back and waited with her until they took her in. She was pretty shaken up."

"Oh, I wish we were there. My poor girl. But I'm glad George's doctor refused to agree to our trip down there."

"Don't worry. Acacia won't be alone. I'm staying the night with her. She just doesn't know it yet. She won't be able to take care of Bobby. I don't think she realizes that. I read up on her surgery after she called me, and she could have complications. I'll be sure she takes care of herself."

"Noah, thank you. Thank you for everything."

"No thanks necessary. I'm glad to help, Rebecca. Listen, I'll call when she's out of recovery and when I see how's she's doing, okay? Don't worry. I'll take care of her."

After he hung up, he strode back into the waiting room and sat down. Waiting was one of the hardest things for him. He'd never been good at it. He preferred to be on the move, accomplishing something. He'd always been an overachiever, even in school. Sitting around while Acacia was in surgery ground against his raw nerves.

He sat until he couldn't stand it any longer, then got up and started pacing again. Acacia had to see this his way. She couldn't be on her own tonight. She could get blood clots. She could start bleeding again. She just shouldn't be alone. But, forget all that. No way should she use her arm to push Bobby around—or use the Hoyer lift or roll her brother around in bed and change his diaper. It would all be too strenuous for her. Not to mention painful.

In fact, she shouldn't be on her own tomorrow. Why hadn't he considered it? He'd have to make arrangements for that, too. He checked his watch again. An hour and twenty minutes. Okay, any time now.

The door opened, and a nurse came out, but she called a gentleman on the other side of the room. Damn. He dialed another number but stayed inside.

Jenny picked up quickly. "Any news, Noah?"

"Not yet. But I wanted to ask you something. Can you free up some time over the next few days to stay with Acacia? I know you have classes on Monday, but in between those. I want her to take it easy."

"Sure. How about I make a list of times I can be here? I'll have it ready when you get home. Okay?"

"That would be wonderful. Thanks, Jen." This was shaping up. He hoped Acacia would see the wisdom in the idea of having help around for a while. She'd be sore, and her tissues would need time to heal. He could stop by and get Bobby out of bed the first few days, then put him back in bed in the evenings. After that, she should be okay. Her recuperation wouldn't be such a problem if it weren't for her brother. He was a big, heavy man, and it took strength to care for him. Strength Acacia didn't have right now.

Just then, her surgeon came out and called his name. He strode over.

"Everything went fine. We removed the lump and some tissue around it, along with several nodes. She's in recovery now. I didn't have to take the breast, so we're on track for her treatment plan."

No mastectomy. Thank God. She'd been so scared about that. "When will you know the biopsy results?"

"My staff will call her for an appointment, and she'll come in next week. It doesn't take long."

"Okay. Can I go back now?"

The doctor smiled. "Someone will come get you in a few minutes."

Noah thanked him and sat down. He'd hoped for biopsy results now. Didn't they have someone in this hospital who could look at the slides? It was criminal making Acacia wait until next week. She'd be a nervous wreck. He crossed his leg, wagging his foot nervously. What was taking them so long? He needed to be back there with her. He got up and started pacing again.

Twenty-five minutes later, a nurse came to the door and called his name.

Stopping mid-stride, he grabbed Acacia's bag and raced to her. "That's me. Is she awake?"

"Yes, sir. Come this way."

Noah followed her back through winding corridors. They obviously weren't going to the same place as before. They finally stopped before a series of small rooms.

The nurse said, "She'll stay here for an hour or two. We want to be sure there's no unusual bleeding or other side effects before we send her home." She opened the door.

The stark white room was very small with no window. It was barely large enough for the gurney and the hard plastic chair for Noah, though it did have a TV on the wall, which was turned down low.

Acacia lay with her eyes closed. She didn't stir when they came in.

The nurse said, "The doctor put a drain in. Apparently, she had a lot of leakage, so we'll check her bandages before she leaves today. Be sure those ice packs stay in place. I'll be back in a little while. Just poke your head out if you need anything."

Pulling the chair close to the bed, he eased Acacia's hand into his grasp. She didn't move, and she was so pale. The dark circles under her eyes appeared drawn with charcoal. Her beautiful lips had lost their natural pink color. Thick bandages on her surgical site raised the sheet higher on that side of her chest. What must she be feeling now? Had she been awake enough yet to understand the surgery results? He squeezed her hand.

A few seconds later, she squeezed his hand in return.

Good, she was coming around.

"Noah?"

"I'm here, Acacia. You okay?"

"Am I okay?"

"Oh, you don't remember?"

"No."

"No mastectomy." He told her everything the doctor had explained, including that they had gone ahead and removed several nodes. "So you'll know what you're looking at next week."

She sighed, her eyes still closed. Then she reached up to her surgical site and knocked the ice packs off.

He grabbed them and gently laid them back in place. "You hurting?"

"Some," she murmured. "When can we leave?"

"We'll be here a couple of hours. Just rest. They want to make sure you're A-OK before we go home."

"Right."

"That TV bothering you?"

"Yes."

"I'll turn it off."

In the silence that followed, Noah held her hand, lending her his strength to face the pain that would follow when the anesthesia wore off. The doctor had probably numbed the surgery sites, and he hoped that might carry her for a while longer. She looked so small and frail tucked into the gurney.

The nurse came in and pulled down the sheet, checking the bandages. So far, they looked fine. She snapped the gown up and left again, saying she'd be back in a little while.

Acacia seemed more alert.

"Do you need anything?" Even in her groggy state, he was looking into the most stunning pair of soft brown eyes he'd ever seen. This woman was everything he wanted, everything he needed, and everything he couldn't have right now.

She licked her lips. "I'm thirsty."

"I'll be right back." He stepped outside the door and found their nurse coming out of another one of the tiny rooms. "Ma'am, may I have a cup of water? She wants a drink."

Though obviously busy, she smiled. "I'll be right there."

He reentered the room and sat down, taking Acacia's hand again.

She squeezed his fingers.

Warmth spread through him. Was there a chink in her armor? Was she opening up to him now? He hoped so. It was so hard being right next to her, yet having her wall set firmly between them. He covered her hand with his free one, hoping she felt his protection. She didn't have to worry about one little thing. All she had to do was get better.

He realized he hadn't called her parents. Dialing the number, he spoke softly when her mom answered. "Hi, Rebecca. She's out of surgery. Everything went fine, though we won't know the biopsy results until next week. We're in a recovery room for the next couple of hours, then I'll take her home. She's drowsing in and out right now. I'll ask her to call you later on tonight when she feels like talking, okay?"

Next, he texted the same information to Jenny and to the number that Acacia had given him for Sarah. Feeling better now that everyone was informed, he clasped Acacia's hand and leaned back, closing his eyes.

The nurse came in and set a pitcher of ice water and a cup on the table. She pulled the sheet down. "How are we doing? Are you hurting, honey?"

Acacia gave her a weak smile. "I am some. Yes."

"You'll be out of here soon, and the doc's ordered pain meds for you. Fill them on the way home, hon."

Noah stared at the bandages. Though they were inches thick, large patches of bloody fluid discolored them. She really was leaking a bunch.

The nurse clucked her tongue. "We'll need a bandage change before you go. I'll send some dressings home with you, but be sure to buy supplies when you pick up your prescription."

The nurse left, and Noah squeezed Acacia's hand. "It's okay. She said earlier that the doc knew you were leaking quite a bit. That's why he put a drain in. Do you remember that?"

Acacia shook her head no.

When the nurse came back in, she reassured Acacia. "Now, I don't want you to worry about this drainage. It's a lot, sure. But, it's not too much. I wouldn't let you go home if it was. And you're leaving after we take care of this. I'll start your paperwork as soon as I'm finished."

#

Within an hour, Noah was pulling his truck up to the doors of the hospital, where the nurse was waiting with Acacia in a wheelchair.

He got out and opened the passenger door.

The nurse wheeled Acacia close and helped her stand. No way would she be able to hoist herself into the lifted truck.

Clasping her waist, he raised her up as she threw an arm around his neck and let out a squeak. Once she was on the seat, he buckled her belt and pulled on the shoulder harness. "That hurting you?"

She shook her head.

"Okay, we're ready to roll. Sit back and relax. We'll be home soon."

She slept all the way to the house.

He was glad of it. She should rest all afternoon.

When they arrived, he helped her down and grabbed her bag. "You okay to walk to the door?"

Rolling her eyes at him, she said, "Yes."

He grinned. "Okay, tough girl. Let's go." He held her arm as they ascended the ramp. Taking her keys, he unlocked the door.

Jenny hopped up from the couch. "Oh, Acacia. How are you?"

"Okay. How did everything go?"

"Great. You never have to worry about Bobby and me. Can I help you with anything?"

Noah said, "Maybe you can help her change into a nightgown and get into bed?" He looked Acacia in the eyes. "Don't yell at me, but I asked Jenny to stay for a while longer. I'm heading home to feed the stock and pack some clothes. Then I'll be back. You won't be up to handling Bobby yet. I'll do that for you."

She pressed her lips together, her eyes settling on several things in the room, ending up on her brother. Then she turned back to him. "Thank you, Noah. I expect you're right."

Jenny took her arm and they walked toward the bedroom.

That had certainly gone more easily than he'd expected it to. He smiled as he headed to the door.

* * *

Acacia drifted near sleep, yet still aware of the soft sounds of Jenny and Bobby talking in the other room. Noah would pick up her pain pills and medical supplies while he was out. Noah... His hand anchoring her safely through her surgery prep had kept her calm. She frowned slightly. As calm as possible considering she'd faced losing a breast.

Bobo walked in and lumbered over to the side of the bed. His big brown eyes stared into hers for a moment, and she could swear he understood that she was in pain. He rested his head on her belly for a few moments, standing perfectly still. She stroked his face with her right hand. Then he laid down beside the bed, a long sigh accompanying the soft thump of his body hitting the floor.

She smiled as slow warmth crawled through her sore chest, despite the ice pack that Noah had refilled before he left. He'd said she was beautiful. That she'd be beautiful even if she had only one breast. That had thrilled her and hurt her at the same time. Why couldn't he be the man for her? Why couldn't he handle everything her life entailed? Why, oh why, did she have to be alone?

She sighed, and pain lanced through her surgical sites. It seemed that Noah could handle things that happened to her. Her, singular. It was just her life with Bobby that he didn't want to deal with.

Having him beside her today, holding her hand, lending his support, had brought back how badly she wanted him in her life. It had only made things worse. The man had made it clear before that he couldn't deal with her problems. He'd pulled away from her. How long would it be before he turned tail and ran?

She couldn't go through that again. No, she *wouldn't* go through that again. She'd *never* be that broken woman again. Bobby needed her strong, not wrecked by some cowardly man who couldn't face responsibility. Tears leaked from her eyes, wetting the pillow. She would have to go it alone.

Chapter Eleven

The room was dim. Was it evening? How long had she slept? Acacia lifted her arm toward the alarm clock and winced in pain, moaning. She'd forgotten and tried to use her left side, where her surgery had been.

Noah walked through the door. "You're awake. How are you feeling?"

He must have been listening for her. "Do I have to answer that?"

He chuckled. "I'll bet you'd like to go to the bathroom, huh?"

Now that he mentioned it... "Yeah, that sounds good."

"Let me help you sit up." Slipping his arm beneath her shoulders, he lifted her to a sitting position.

He smelled fresh and of the cologne she liked so much. He'd showered while he was away. Her heart galloped, and she reined it back. Enough of that. "Thanks. I've got this."

"Let's take it easy. Don't push it." Pulling the covers from her legs, he eased her feet to the ground while supporting her shoulders.

She sucked in her lower lip. He was good at this. That hadn't hurt, although her breast was aching pretty badly right now. Where had he learned to be so gentle?

He put his arm around her and brought her to a standing position. "Lead on. I'm with you."

She lifted the corner of her mouth in a half smile. "Oh Lord, the indignities."

Once at the bathroom door, she looked him in the eye. "You are *not* coming in."

He pressed his lips together, narrowing his eyes.

"Seriously, you're not. I'd die first. You can wait outside." She shut the door, fast, before he could come up with an argument.

Actually, she could definitely have used him. She hurt like hell getting on and off the toilet. But there were some things a woman couldn't face, and having a sexy man help her pee was one of them.

He stood waiting, arms crossed, leaning against the wall, when she opened the door. Pushing off, he caught her arm. "I think you should head back to bed, don't you? It's been a long day."

Actually, that sounded like a great idea. It'd be about all she could do to make it that far. "We're on the same page there." When he slid his arm around her again, she couldn't help it; she pulled in a lungful of his wonderful smell and leaned against him. Maybe just this once she'd enjoy his touch.

He eased her back into bed, as gently as before, and covered her up. "Do you want to watch TV, or is quiet better?

She sighed. "No TV, please. I'm tired."

"Are you hungry?"

"Not really."

"Do you think you could try to eat if I brought you something? You haven't had anything all day."

If she was going to get her strength back, she did need to eat. "Sure, thanks, Noah."

He came back a little while later with chicken noodle soup, crackers, and some juice. He held the plate so that she could feed herself. It was strange, being waited on like this, but it was also gentle and kind and went straight to her heart.

When she'd finished the soup and had eaten most of the crackers, he handed her the juice and took the dishes to the kitchen. She eased back down onto the pillows, feeling more like herself.

A few minutes later, he walked back into the room. "Are you up to calling your parents?"

Damn, she'd forgotten all about that. What was wrong with her? "Please could you bring me my phone?"

He came back in and handed it to her, then left the room. How did the man know exactly what she needed all the time? It was spooky—like he was tuned into her soul. She chewed on her lip as she dialed. Okay, maybe it was kind of awesome, too.

Her mom picked up, and Acacia said, "Hi, I'm sorry it took so long for me to call you. I fell asleep."

"Oh my goodness, of course you did. Noah kept us posted. I'm so glad you could rest, honey. How are you feeling?"

He'd called them while she was sleeping? That was nice. "Well, I hurt, but I'm sure that's normal. The pain medicine will help. How's Dad?"

Her mom sighed. "Acacia, I don't know what to do with him. He went to the doctor, all right. But he won't do anything the doctor says. Doc took one listen to his heart and wanted to call an ambulance and send him to the hospital in Wichita Falls. That's how bad it is. Do you think that stubborn man would go? He told doc that he has heifers due to calve right now, and that he'll go in a few days. Doc told him he couldn't wait, and your dad just waved his hand and got up and left. I swear, Acacia, I'm worried sick. If doc thinks the problem is that serious, George needs to go."

Acacia's heart pounded. Why was her dad so freaking stubborn? This sounded life-threatening, and he was ignoring his doctor completely. "Is Dad there now?"

"No, honey. He's still out."

"Well, you tell him I want to talk to him when he gets in. He's going to hear it from me."

"Oh, Acacia, I hope you can talk some sense into him. He's always been stubborn, but this? I just don't understand what he's thinking. He's refusing to deal with it."

"I love you, Momma. Try not to worry, okay?"

Her mom sighed. "Listen to me, here I am putting all this stress on you, and you just had surgery. I ought to be whipped. I'm sorry, honey."

"No, Mom, I'm sorry you're having to put up with Daddy acting like this. You're too weak to deal with him right now, and he should remember that. Just hang in there. I'll try to sort it out."

By the time she got off the phone, her breast was pounding with every heartbeat. Noah must have been listening for her to hang up, because he came back into the room. She licked her dry lips. "Noah? Is it time for my pain medicine yet?"

A dark-pink flush crawled up his neck. "Dammit. Some nurse I am. It's past time for it. Let me get it for you."

He returned quickly with her pill and set the bottle by the bed.

She took it with some of the juice. The poor man looked so guilty. She reached for his hand. "I'm fine. Don't worry about it."

As he sat on the edge of the bed, he said, "Bobby's had dinner, and we've done his therapy. Does he have a bedtime routine?"

She wrinkled her nose. "Bedtime stories?"

He grinned. "I can do bedtime stories. Does he pick them?"

Relieved, she nodded. "Hold up each book from his basket, and he'll choose one when he sees what he wants. Don't let him take advantage of you. You decide how many you want to read. On my best nights, I read three."

He laughed. "Okay. No problem. What else?"

She explained the tooth-brushing process. "And you know the Hoyer lift routine." She frowned, hardly daring to meet his eyes. "Then there's the diaper. I'm sorry."

"Don't be. I worked in a hospital to put myself through school. Won't be my first diaper."

Relief flooded her and she let out the breath she hadn't known that she was holding. She'd been dreading having him help with her brother, sure he'd be uncomfortable with it. But it seems he wasn't after all. "Bobby doesn't wear pajamas. He never did because he sleeps so hot. When this first happened, we thought maybe he might need them, but he was still the same. So, just the diaper at nighttime. And the covers."

He patted her hand and stood. "I'll check in with you in a little bit. I hope that pain pill starts to work fast."

He'd left her door open. She closed her eyes and listened to the sounds of the two of them as Noah helped Bobby pick out his books, then as he read them to him. And, yes, there were three.

She clutched the covers, weightless. Would she float right off the bed? It could be her pain pill—or was this joy, listening to her brother laugh with Noah as he brushed his teeth? Despite her surgery, this had been a perfect day. Noah had made it that way.

They must have moved into Bobby's room. The hum of the hydraulic lift sounded. He was putting Bobby in his bed. Her brother giggled. What the heck was Noah saying that had Bobby laughing so? In a little while, she heard, "Good night." And, "Okay."

Noah walked back in. "Bobby said to leave his door open. Is that right?"

She grinned. "I usually close it. He wakes up at small noises in the house, so I keep it shut, and he sleeps better that way. He's being nosy because you're here and he doesn't want to miss any of the action. It's okay, though. You can close the door after he goes to sleep."

Noah sat on the edge of the bed and clasped her hand.

Squeezing his fingers, she sensed their closeness tonight. "Thanks for all you've done today."

He looked into her eyes. "You're welcome. I meant it when I said I'm here for you, for whatever you need, Acacia." He increased the pressure on her fingers slightly. "Will you tell me something? After your surgery, your surgeon said that you should be on track for your treatment plan. I was just wondering what that was."

She sighed. Today had only been the first hurdle. She hadn't let herself think about the next step much. "I may need radiation therapy, assuming that the lump, and maybe the nodes, come back cancerous, as they expect they will. I'll probably see an oncologist. I'll talk more about that this coming week when I see my surgeon again. Depending on what they find in the lymph nodes, I may need chemotherapy, too, after the radiation."

Noah nodded. "So a lot depends on these test results."

"Yeah." This talk was making everything all too real. Her pulse had picked up.

"Would you like me to go with you to this appointment?"

God, it would be great to have him there when she got the news, whatever it was. She pressed her lips together. No, she needed to handle this herself. She couldn't expect other people to put their life on hold while she went through treatment. "Oh, no, I'll be okay. But thank you."

He waited for a few seconds. "The offer still stands if you change your mind." Then he stood, his gaze roving over her, the bedside table, the window, which he'd already checked. "You want anything before I hit the sack?"

"Noah, I was thinking. I'll be fine in the morning. You don't need to stay—"

"Nonsense. You'll feel worse than ever. And there's Bobby to think of. Now you close those eyes and sleep. Rest is the best medicine. I'll be in here in five hours to give you more pain meds." He turned off the lamp and strode out, leaving the door open.

What he lacked in bedside manner he made up for in good intentions. He was right. She would most likely be worse in the morning, and she owed it to Bobby to keep help available.

The sliding door opened and closed. He must be letting Bobo outside to potty.

In a minute, the bathroom door opened and closed. It was so intimate, having him here in her home, changing clothes in her bathroom. What would he sleep in? Did he wear pajamas?

Or would it only be a pair of shorts? The vision that produced caused her heart rate to climb. She smiled at herself. And then she stopped. What was she doing? What had his words been that night? Oh, that's right: *I just can't*. The days of having a man in her life were gone.

The sliding door opened and, like her heart must, closed a last time.

* * *

Noah turned off the bathroom light and shut the door quietly. That pain pill should be working. With any luck, Acacia would already be asleep. He drew a glass of water from the kitchen faucet and brought it into the living room, setting it on the end table. Grabbing the throw from the back of the couch, he lay down against his pillow. He hadn't slept in a T-shirt and shorts since his college days, when his roommate had girls traipsing into their room at all hours. He would miss the freedom of sleeping in his briefs. He'd already made a round of the house. All the doors and windows were locked. Acacia had smiled when he'd checked the window in her room.

She was different today, in a good way. As though she were softening toward him. He really hoped that they could talk tomorrow about what was wrong between them. This strain—the distance between them—hurt too much. The more he was around her, the more he wanted to be close to her. The look on her face today when she'd talked about the mastectomy... Well, it had nearly broken his heart. As if her losing a breast would make any difference to him. She was beautiful on the inside. That was what he loved. Blinking hard, he sucked in a breath. Loved? Was that what this thing he had for her was?

He reached up and turned off the lamp. Of course he loved her. That was what all this yanking and pulling on his heart had been. He and Acacia really had to talk. Her pain meds should start working, and then maybe she'd feel up to it. Right now, she was too weak to do anything.

Tomorrow, he'd be around all day. If there was a way, he would clear things up between them, once and for all.

* * *

Bobby's happy voice woke Noah. He smiled as he listened to him talking to himself in bed. So, the guy was an early riser, huh? He swung his legs to the carpet and padded into Bobby's room. "Good morning, buddy. How are you?"

Bobby laughed and rolled his head side to side, his arms flailing. "Noah. Noah. You're here."

"Yep. You ready to get up and watch cartoons?"

"Where's 'Cacia?"

"She's in bed. She's still not feeling good. I'm taking care of you today."

Bobby grinned. "Okay, Noah."

"You hang tight for a few minutes, and I'll be back to get you up, all right?"

Noah made some coffee and checked on Acacia. She was still asleep, so he shut her door. After a quick trip to the bathroom, he joined Bobby again. "Okay, big guy, let's get you ready for the day." He let Bobby decide on some clothes, then changed his diaper. It took strength to get him dressed, and the process gave Noah a new appreciation for what Acacia went through each day.

Using the lift, he settled Bobby into his wheelchair. "Are you hungry for breakfast yet?"

"No. I want cartoons."

"Are you thirsty?"

"Yeah, I want milk. Please."

"Thanks for saying *please*, buddy. I'll bring you some." After wheeling him in front of the TV and helping him find his favorite show, Noah served himself some coffee and brought Bobby his milk. The guy was thirsty. He drank most of the cup before he let Noah set it on the table.

Jenny was coming over for a few hours so that Noah could go home and feed. Along with caring for Acacia, he would have a busy day. He took a swallow of coffee. Would she feel better this morning? Or, as he'd predicted, would she be worse? Hopefully, keeping her full of pain medication during the night had helped. He'd hated waking her to give her the pill, but he couldn't let pain get a hold on her.

By the time he'd fed Bobby breakfast, it was time to check Acacia again. He opened the door a crack and she turned her head, so he walked on in. "You're awake. How are you this morning?"

His eyes widened as he grew close to her and saw the tears pooling in her eyes.

She attempted to sit up, then lay back down with a whimper.

"Let's give you a pain pill." He shook one out of the bottle and handed her the glass of water by the bed, helping her lift her head to take it.

As he sat down beside her, the problem became obvious. Her bandages were saturated with serous fluid, and it had gotten on her gown. She must be hurting something awful. Grasping her hand, he said, "Honey, I'm sorry. Where are your clean gowns?"

She bit her lip and pointed to the dresser on the side of the room. He found one that should work and came back to the bed, laying it at the foot. "Hold on a couple of minutes. I'll be right back."

Nodding, she closed her eyes.

When he returned, he had a bowl of hot soapy water with him. He located two washcloths and a hand towel and brought the bandaging supplies to the bedside.

Acacia opened her eyes when he sat on the bed, noticing all of his preparations. Her eyes grew round and she said, her voice quavering, "Oh no, I can do this myself. I'm a nurse, you know. I don't need any help."

Gently, he said, "Acacia, you do. There's no way you can bandage yourself, at least not well. And, while you try, you'll be in pain. Remember I said I worked in a hospital? I've got this. Now let me get you cleaned up."

She squeezed her eyes shut and nodded her head.

Noah eased her gown above her hips and helped her to sit up. Between her swollen breast and the thick pad of dressings, her gown was difficult to take off, but he eventually got it over her head. She was naked but for her panties.

Acacia turned her head away, her eyes still closed, red creeping up her face.

As he laid her back down, he murmured, "Easy now, I'll take your dressing off." He started at the edges of the tape and drew it slowly away from her skin. It took time as it was a large bandage and there were several layers. As the last of it peeled away, he stuffed the soiled remains into the bag he'd brought for that purpose.

She still held her eyes closed, looking pale and fragile.

She was beautiful and so vulnerable, lying there waiting for him to care for her. This must be so overwhelming. He said softly, "I'm going to clean you now. The water's warm. I'll be careful."

Dipping the cloth in the soapy water, he squeezed the excess out and gently dabbed at the bloody fluid on her breast. The mess was especially bad at the drain site. Trying to exert the least amount of pressure, he dipped a clean part of the cloth in more water and moved on, keeping clear of the stitches. Her eyes had relaxed. He must be doing okay. Lifting her breast, he cleaned under it and all the way around to her back, where the pink fluid had run. He picked up a new cloth and wet it, then went over all of the areas again. Finally, he dried everything with the clean hand towel. "I did the best I can, but with you being a nurse, I'm sure you'll spot something wrong with the job I'm doing," he said with a smile.

She shook her head, but didn't open her eyes. "It'll be fine. Thanks for your help."

Clasping her hand for a few seconds, he let her rest.

She squeezed his hand back.

He wanted so much to care for her. What he was doing filled a deep need in him. His heart, which had hurt more each day that she'd pushed him away, found peace in these simple tasks.

"I'll put your dressing on now. Don't worry, I'll be careful." He'd examined what he'd taken off, so he was able to recreate it with the bandages he'd bought and the non-stick surgical tape. Picking up her gown, he said, "Last step. Let's get you dressed."

She turned her head to look at him and tried to sit up, but winced.

He frowned. "Acacia, will you quit that? Let me help you." Sliding his arm around her back, he helped her sit up and slipped the gown over her head. After she put her right arm in, he lifted her left arm and pushed it through, laying it back down at her side. Then he helped her lie down again. Standing, he raised her hips up and pulled her gown down around her thighs and over her butt. Once he slid the covers up over her, he inspected his handiwork.

The corners of her mouth tilted up in a weak smile. "Thanks, Noah."

"Of course. I'll fill those ice packs again, see if we can make more of that swelling go away."

The poor woman looked terrible this morning. The bruising in her breast was starting to come to the surface, and there would be a lot of discoloration. The ice packs should help.

He filled the ice bags at the freezer. With Acacia this sore and weak, would they be able to talk things over today? The two of them had to work through this problem somehow. What would it take to make her see that?

He took the ice packs in and laid them gently across her chest. She looked at him, an unreadable expression on her face. What was she thinking? He brushed a tendril of hair from her forehead. "I'm fixing you some breakfast. You need something in your stomach after taking that pain pill, okay?"

She nodded. "How's Bobby doing?"

"He woke up happy today."

"He usually does. Some days, he's my inspiration."

Did she have any idea how special she was? How much he admired her? Her courage was *his* inspiration. He was surer now than ever before that he loved her and wanted to spend the rest of his life taking care of her. "I'll be back in a little while. Don't go away."

She rolled her eyes.

Later, he came in with breakfast. He set the tray he'd found in the kitchen on her lap and the milk on the nightstand.

"Thanks. I'm getting up after I eat. I can't lie in bed all day."

"That sounds great. Why don't you take a bath? Jenny will be here shortly. Just don't get your bandages wet. I'll head home and feed, then I'll be back later." When she started to speak, he said, "I'm coming back. No way are you in any shape to handle Bobby yet."

She pursed her lips and nodded. "Okay. Thanks, Noah."

* * *

Jenny supported Acacia as she eased down into the steaming bath. Though she was feeling better, she still wasn't able to use the left side of her upper body, so her balance was a bit off. Tomorrow, she'd start using it in little bits. She had to. But today it was still excruciating to move her arm. Lying back, she was careful to keep the water level below her bandages. She liked her baths hot, and this one was. Closing her eyes, she let the soothing heat seep into her.

Having Noah change her dressing had been embarrassing, but he'd been so professional about the whole thing that she'd almost forgotten who he was. Almost. His touch had been so light, so gentle. With her painful breast, she'd dreaded the ordeal of a bandage change, but with his careful hands, it hadn't hurt too much. In the end, what she'd felt was cared for, almost cherished. Her miracle cowboy had that way about him.

Her phone rang, and she picked it up. *Sarah*. Putting it on speaker, she said, "Hi. What are you doing calling me this time of day?"

"I had some time before a meeting and wanted to see how you're feeling. Are you okay to talk?"

"I'm actually enjoying a hot bath. I'd love to chat."

"Where's Noah?"

She brought her friend up to speed, including the scoop about the uncomfortable dressing change.

"I think that's so sweet. I told you I liked this guy."

Acacia wet a washcloth and dribbled water down her arm. "I'm pretty confused. I can't square what Noah said to me before he rushed out the door that night with the man who went through every step of my surgery with me and who has cared for Bobby, including changing his diapers. Have I been wrong about him, Sarah? If so, what the hell happened that night?"

"Baby, you've got to talk to the man. Listen to your bestie now. Talk. To. Noah."

Acacia covered her face with the hot washcloth. Her friend was right. She had to speak to him. Pulling it off, she rinsed it in the water. "He makes me feel so..." She tried to put it into words. "He's so gentle with me, but he's strong, too. And I'm stronger when I'm with him. Sarah, the way he touches me...it's like he's afraid I'll break."

"It sounds wonderful, honey."

"It is, and it scares me. I don't want to hope. I can't take being left again." She rubbed her hand over her wet face.

"Noah's not like Johnny, sweetheart. That bastard had no soul."

"How can I trust this? I never saw it coming with Johnny. One day I was ecstatic, getting ready to be married, and the next day I was all alone."

"You can't live the rest of your life in the past. It's time to look forward to the future. You have one, you know. He's been looking you in the face for several months now."

Acacia dropped her washcloth in the water. "I guess I have a lot to think about, huh?"

"Get to it, girl. I expect to hear good news soon. I love you. Got to run."

Acacia finished washing herself the best she could with one arm. Jenny had said to yell when she was ready to get out, so she did. Thank God the young woman was there to help her put on an oversized T-shirt and some leggings. What a joke it was that she'd thought she didn't need Noah's help anymore. No way was she up to pushing Bobby's wheelchair. She'd nearly cried like a baby getting dressed.

The bath, and maybe her talk with Sarah, had energized her. She headed out to the living room to check on her brother. He had one of his stuffed dinosaurs in his lap and was watching cartoons. "Hey, Bobby, how's it going?" Leaning down slowly, she gave him a kiss.

He beamed. "'Cacia. You're back."

She stroked his cheek. His brilliant smile always raised her spirits. She'd really missed him. "Do you know how much I love you?"

He nodded his head vigorously. "Uh-huh, the whole sky full."

"That's right, brother, and don't you forget it."

"Okay, 'Cacia."

"Can I help you with anything?" Jenny asked.

"Oh, would you mind bringing me some iced tea out on the porch? I'd appreciate it."

Jenny patted her arm. "You go sit yourself down, and I'll bring it right out."

Acacia settled down into her favorite chair, its padded seat molded to her behind from all of the wonderful hours she'd spent in it. She could always relax and do her best thinking out here.

Jenny stepped out and handed her a glass of tea, then, as if sensing her need for solitude, went back in, quietly shutting the door.

Acacia took a sip and let the cool fluid dribble down her throat. Images flashed before her, and Noah was in every one. It had come down to one essential thing. Could she trust him?

* * *

Jenny answered the door, and one look at her face set Noah's heart racing. What had happened? Was Acacia bleeding again? He pushed his way inside, causing Jenny to take a quick step back, and asked, "What's wrong? Where's Acacia?"

Jenny put her finger to her lips. "Follow me," she whispered, as she led him to the kitchen.

What was wrong? He didn't want to follow her. He wanted to find Acacia.

Jenny turned to face him. "Acacia's out on the porch, but she's had terrible news. Her father passed away. Bobby doesn't know yet."

Her father was dead? Oh God, she must be devastated. He turned on his heel, striding through the living room.

"Hi, Noah," Bobby said.

He couldn't ignore Bobby, though everything inside him screamed at him to run to Acacia's side.

Kneeling beside Bobby's chair, he said, "Hey, buddy. How's it going?"

"Can you play with me?"

"Sure, in a little while. I need to talk to Acacia now, though. Will you be all right for a few minutes longer?"

"Okay, Noah," Bobby replied through pouting lips.

Noah patted his shoulder and strode to the back door.

Acacia sat in her chair, head bowed. For once, Bobo had left his master's side and followed Acacia outside. His big head rested on her thigh, as if to give her solace.

Noah slipped his arm around the big dog's shoulders and knelt beside her, tilting her chin up.

She looked at him through tear-filled eyes, her lips trembling.

"Honey, I'm so sorry." He grasped her shoulders and stood, lifting her into his arms. Brushing her hair away from her cheek, he kissed it. "Shush, I'm here."

She clutched his shirt, digging her face into him. "He didn't call, and I forgot to. If I'd talked to him, he would have gone to the hospital. Noah, why didn't I call?"

Sobs wracked her body, and he knew that had to be hurting her breast. He cradled her head, kissing her forehead. "You don't know that. George was a stubborn man, and you've had all you could do to take care of yourself, sweetheart. Please don't do this."

She shook her head. "No, he would have listened to me. Dad always did."

He cupped her face in his hands and made her look at him. "Acacia, nobody can make anyone do what they don't want to do. And your dad wanted to be there with his heifers. Do you honestly think he'd leave them if he thought there'd be trouble?"

She lowered her eyes. "No, probably not."

"So you couldn't have changed his mind. He made his choice, and this time it caught up with him."

Acacia started crying again, and he wrapped his arms around her, careful not to hold too tight. Her every sob hurt his soul. She was breaking his heart.

In time, she quieted and pulled back.

He handed her his handkerchief. "What do you need? I'll do anything you want me to."

"God, I don't know. I can't think. When Mom called, the ambulance had just gotten there. Then the sheriff drove up." She sniffed. Her hands shook as she wiped her nose. "I told Mom to call me back when everybody left and she could talk." She sobbed once and covered her mouth with a shaky hand.

He put his arm around her. "Let's sit down." After she was settled, he sat in the other chair.

She squeezed her hand into a fist, her eyes downcast. "Dad was in the barn with those damn heifers. Mom expected him for lunch. After a while, when he didn't come in, she went down to check on him. He'd just pulled a calf. The puller was on the ground next to him, and the heifer was still tied up. The baby had gotten up on its own and gone to its momma. You know what hard work pulling a calf is. The effort must've been too much for his heart." She sucked in her quivering lip.

"When you're ready to handle the arrangements, I'd be glad to make some calls, if you'd rather not do that. Or I can just be here with you. Whatever you need."

She took a deep breath. "Thank you, Noah." Then her eyes widened. "Oh, no. Bobby. How will I tell Bobby?" Her eyes filled with tears, and she put her fingers to her lips to stop their trembling.

Noah reached for her hand. "I'll help you tell him. You won't have to do it alone. Keep it simple. Just figure out what you want to say first, okay?"

She sniffed and nodded.

"Why don't I bring you some fresh tea while you think?"

Once inside, he shook his head. Why hadn't he reminded her to call when her father hadn't called her back? He'd over-heard her side of the conversation. It had slipped his mind, too, and now she carried that guilt. She shouldn't, but how could you tell a grieving daughter that? He'd call Rebecca later, tell her how sorry he was. God, how much more could Acacia take? Life was just dealing her one heavy blow after another, and she was so weak right now. But she wouldn't be alone. He'd see to that. As he poured her tea, he was more determined than ever to care for her. Not just now, but always.

He walked back out on the porch and set her tea down in front of her. She seemed a little more composed.

The corner of her mouth turned up. "Thank you, Noah, for everything."

Her eyes, red from crying, wrenched his heart. He wanted to take her in his arms and make everything bad go away. "I wouldn't be anywhere else."

She sipped her tea and looked out into the yard. "I can't believe this is happening. I always knew someday I'd lose my parents, but I'm not prepared." Her bottom lip quivered again.

"I know. I dread the day it happens to me." He clasped her hand, stroking her with his thumb.

With a gentle squeeze, he asked, "Would you tell me something? I get it that you've been angry with me. I'm so sorry I hurt you—that I came on to you so hard. But why wouldn't you talk to me? I thought we meant more to each other than that." He held his breath, hoping for once that she would break her silence and let him in.

She drew her brows together in a puzzled frown. "What? You thought I was upset because you came on to me?" Shaking her head, she let out a short laugh. "No way, I was totally into you that night." She stared at him, as if measuring her words. "After what you said, I thought you didn't want the burden Bobby represented in your life. I couldn't figure it out; I mean, you already knew I was Bobby's caregiver. Why would you suddenly have a problem with it? It felt like what happened with my fiancé all over again, and I couldn't believe it. I felt so stupid."

"Honey, of course, I know you and Bobby are a package deal, and one I'd happily accept. I thought I had scared you; moved too fast. I knew it had been a long time since you'd been with a man." He grinned ruefully and shook his head. "Lord, what a mess. I hope you believe me now that I would never turn my back on you, especially because of Bobby."

"The past couple of days have made me realize that. Thank you so much for all you've done. I couldn't have managed without your help and without Jenny being here. How I thought I could function alone—especially with Bobby—I'll never know."

In a little while, after she'd finished her tea, she said, "I guess I know what to say. Shall we go in?"

He helped her stand, laying his arm around her shoulders as they walked inside. When they entered the living room, he turned Bobby's wheelchair around, then muted the TV. Kneeling before the chair, he rested his hand on Bobby's leg.

Acacia got down on her knees next to Noah. She clasped Bobby's hand and looked him in the eyes. "Brother, I have something very sad to tell you. Daddy died and went to heaven today."

Noah wrapped his arm around her, offering her his strength. How terrible she must have felt when she'd thought he hadn't wanted Bobby in his life. And now she had to help her brother understand her father's death.

Bobby drew his brows together. "You cried, 'Cacia? Your eyes are sad."

"Yes, Bobby, I'm really sad right now. I won't see Daddy anymore until it's my turn to go to heaven. Do you understand that?"

"What?"

"Dad's in heaven now, Bobby. We won't see him again until we die and go to heaven. That's a long time. It's why I'm sad. I miss Daddy." She choked on the last word and turned to Noah.

Pulling her closer, he kissed her cheek, then squeezed Bobby's knee. "It's okay for you to feel sad now, too."

Bobby looked from Acacia to Noah and back again. "I want Daddy, 'Cacia." His face crumpled. "Don't be sad, 'Cacia." He ended in a wail.

Acacia stood and hugged him, tears of her own falling on his shoulder. "Bobby, I want Daddy too. But we'll be okay. In a while, we'll feel happy again."

Noah stood. Bobby didn't understand. He only knew his sister was hurting. Cupping the back of Bobby's neck, he kissed the top of his head. The guy, even with all of his challenges, had such a good heart.

Acacia took a deep breath, and Bobby sniffed loudly. "'Cacia, don't cry."

Acacia pulled back and wiped his cheeks.

"Noah?" Bobby said.

"Uh-huh?"

"Would you be my daddy now?"

Noah blinked. And took a breath, exhaling while he considered his response. "Bobby, I'll always be here for you." He looked at Acacia, whose eyes were wide, staring at him. "What do you think about that?"

"Will you be—here for him, always?" she asked quietly.

"Yes, in any way you'll let me, I will. What do you say?"

She smiled, and it was like the sun shone in the room. "I think you've said it all."

He pulled her to her feet and into his arms. "Acacia, I love you. And I'm asking now before you change your mind. Will you marry me and make me Bobby's daddy?"

Chapter Twelve

Noah stood beside Ronnie and Bobby in the church in Howelton, the North Texas town where Acacia had grown up. Since the dais was two feet above the floor, it had taken Noah, Ronnie, and Acacia's Uncle Dan to lift her brother up there for the ceremony. He was the ring bearer and damn proud of it. The satin pillow with the rings lay on his lap.

Large rose-pink and cream-colored flowers with big loops of cream ribbon adorned the ends of each pew. The strong smell of lilies from a flower arrangement on the table behind them filled the sanctuary. Organ music played in the background as people in the pews talked quietly among themselves. Any minute now. Noah could feel the pulse throbbing in his neck.

He'd waited so long for this day. After her biopsy had come back positive for stage one breast cancer, Acacia had completed radiation therapy but hadn't needed chemo. During that time, she'd planned a simple wedding. In less than three months, she'd sent out invitations and had pulled it all together. He couldn't wait to see her. She'd be gorgeous. No, more than gorgeous. She'd be breathtaking.

Noah caught his mother's eye and smiled. His parents and his brother, Joe, were here. Even his sister, Carolyn, had been able to make it. He'd told his parents they didn't need to come. Howelton was a long trip for Joe to make. Although his mom planned to have a reception at home for his side of the family after their honeymoon, she had insisted on coming to the ceremony. She'd said that she wasn't about to miss her son getting married.

If he'd only known that telling Acacia about Joe could have made such a difference. He'd never guessed that she'd thought that he'd left that night because he considered Bobby too much of a burden. It was crazy how misunderstandings could go on and on when each person assumed they knew exactly what the other was thinking.

He'd always known that someday he'd find the right woman. Although he'd never thought about what his wedding would be like, this simple wedding in Acacia's small hometown church was perfect. And this tight-knit ranching community was his kind of crowd. As the men walked in, they doffed their cowboy hats in respect. Women who hadn't seen Rebecca since George's passing had wrapped her in a hug, and the men had given her a gentle handshake.

Looking around at all the children here today, he realized that he'd never asked Acacia how many she wanted. He thought three was a nice number. Boys and girls both would be great, though as long as they were healthy, he'd be happy. He'd have to ask her about it. Gusting out a breath, he clasped his hands behind his back. What was taking so long?

Ronnie leaned into him. "How're you doing?"

"I'm tired of waiting."

Ronnie grinned. "Hold your horses, partner. She'll be yours soon enough."

Noah smiled back. "I guess a couple more minutes won't hurt." Ronnie would be doing the feeding at the ranch for Noah. He'd also offered to take Bobo home with him. The big dog had greeted Ronnie as if he were a long-lost friend when he'd come to pick him up.

Noah knelt by Bobby and whispered, "You hanging in there, buddy?"

"I'm hungry." Bobby tried to speak softly but wasn't too successful.

"I'll tell your mom when we're done with all this, okay? Acacia will be here in a minute. Do you remember what I told you?"

"Yeah. I got to be quiet. That's my job."

"Right, buddy. You're doing your first job right now—holding my ring for Acacia. I sure appreciate you doing that. You're a great helper."

Bobby laughed. "I'm a great he-helper, Noah."

Just then the organ rang out, the chords of "The Bridal Chorus" from Wagner's Opera *Lohengrin* filling the air. Noah shot to his feet, his gaze locked on the end of the aisle for his first wondrous glimpse of his bride.

* * *

Acacia stepped from the small room at the end of the hallway, "The Bridal Chorus" loud in the familiar church. Her Uncle Dan, who had been waiting patiently for her, smiled and lifted his elbow. Her heart clenched. Tears pooled behind her eyes as she answered his smile. If only her dad were here, today would be perfect. She slipped her hand around her uncle's arm.

Sarah stood ready in front of them, holding Cara's hand. Her basket full of rose petals sent up a wonderful fragrance.

Their little procession moved toward the doors of the church, which stood open, ready for their entry. Acacia had decided on a slow walk down the aisle. She wanted time to acknowledge as many of her friends as possible. It had been more than two long years since she'd seen most of them, and she wanted everyone to know how much she loved them.

Sarah let go of Cara's hand, and the little girl walked ahead, throwing her flower petals out in front of her. The guests smiled, adoring the cute picture she made in her cream and rose taffeta dress and lace tights. Sarah followed, leading them at a sedate pace.

Acacia tightened her grip on her uncle's arm. *Noah.* A nameless rush of heady emotions swept through her. He was magnificent in his black tuxedo. And her brother. You'd never know a childlike mind lived in the handsome young man who stared at her with that great big smile.

She looked to her right, where neighbors she grew up with stood. On her left were two families she'd gone to church with all her life. Midway down the aisle, Jenny beamed at her. How wonderful it was to have the sweet young woman here today. Acacia grinned, locking eyes with as many people as she could. They all made this day special.

Soon, they were at the front of the church, where her mother stood with tears in her eyes. Acacia's heart clutched again. She knew her mom was thinking about her dad too. Acacia mouthed, "I love you."

Her mom smiled through her tears and blew her a kiss.

Her uncle led her up the steps and straight to Noah. She smiled at Bobby, who had a brilliant grin on his face.

"Who gives this woman to be married?" the minister asked.

"I do," her uncle answered. He placed her hand in Noah's, then stepped down off the dais.

She responded instantly to Noah's touch. Excitement, love, and desire nearly overwhelmed her.

"Stand before me as a couple, please," the minister said.

Noah put his hand at her waist and guided her over, smiling down at her.

She squeezed his hand. How could she love him more? His whole heart had been in his eyes, in that smile.

As the minister talked to them about the sanctity and responsibilities of marriage, she imagined being married to Noah in fifty years. It would still be good. This man's soul was true and strong. What a lucky woman she was. All her worry about spending her life alone had been for nothing. She just hadn't met the perfect man yet. She leaned her head into Noah's shoulder and tuned back in to the minister's words. Soon, it was time for their vows.

Noah faced her with a sweet, almost shy, smile. He looked into her eyes as he held the ring to her finger, and said, "I, Noah Rowden, choose you, Acacia Richards, to be my wife. I promise to listen to you and always talk to you, so that no misunderstandings will ever tear us apart."

He smiled bigger, love pouring from his eyes. "I will respect you and love you as my equal. I promise to laugh with you when times are good and endure with you when they're bad. I will always adore, honor, and encourage you. You're my best friend, and I will love you always." He slipped the ring on her finger, then pulled her hand to his lips and kissed it.

His vows overwhelmed her. They were perfect—everything she could have hoped for. Noah understood her heart in a way no one ever had.

Now it was her turn. She prayed that she had captured his needs as well.

Sarah handed her the ring.

Acacia slid the ring to the first knuckle of Noah's finger and looked into his warm, brown eyes. "I, Acacia Richards, take you, Noah Rowden, for my husband, my partner in life, and my one true love. I will cherish our marriage and love you more each day than I did before. I will trust you and respect you, laugh with you and cry with you, loving you faithfully through the good times and bad, regardless of the obstacles we may face together. I give you my hand, my heart, and my love from this day forward, for as long as we both shall live." She smiled into his eyes and slid the ring on his finger.

"In the eyes of God and under the laws of man, I now pronounce you man and wife. You may kiss the bride."

Noah grinned and leaned in, covering her mouth in a kiss that sent her heart racing. Still holding her tight, he lifted her off the ground.

She laughed and clung to his shoulders.

The guests clapped, and the triumphant chords of Mendelssohn's "Wedding March" filled the building.

Noah clasped her hand and led her down the steps.

Guests called out congratulations as they walked back down the aisle, and a sense of overwhelming joy filled her. Her packed bags were in the waiting room. They'd both make a quick change now and leave for the honeymoon from the church. The long black limo Ronnie had hired to drive them all the way to the Dallas airport sat running outside.

Sarah helped Acacia remove the veil and wedding dress and step into the more casual dress and heels she'd packed for the plane.

There was a knock on the door. Ronnie called, "You decent so I can grab those bags?"

Sarah opened the door. "We're ready."

Noah stood behind him, sexy as hell in his ironed shirt and Wranglers. Her heart crashed in a crazy rhythm against her sternum. This man was hers now.

Acacia grinned at him. "I'm ready, Mr. Rowden."

He tipped his hat. "I'm waiting, Mrs. Rowden."

He offered his arm, and they headed toward the church doors.

The bright Texas sun glared in her eyes as guests hurled birdseed at them. Noah curved his arm around her while they ducked and raced to the car. On the curb, she turned and blew a kiss to her mom and a grinning Bobby.

As they drove away, she stared back through the rear window and reached for Noah's hand. She'd left Acacia Richards behind forever. Leaning over, she pulled her husband to her, claiming his mouth hungrily. She was Acacia Rowden now.

Chapter Thirteen

The lights of Venice appeared out of the cloud cover in the distance. Noah reached out and tucked a lock of fallen hair behind Acacia's ear as she slept. The flight from Chicago had been long—more than ten hours. Though it had been tiring, he'd enjoyed it. Seldom did he and Acacia have uninterrupted hours alone. A new contentment had come over him since he'd slipped his ring on her finger. Everything in his life made sense now. He could see the road ahead clearly. He'd needed Acacia, this one particular, very special woman, to make his life perfect.

He covered her slender, capable hand with his. Their honeymoon would be exciting. Neither he nor Acacia had been overseas before. But, more than anything, he looked forward to getting home and starting a life with her at the ranch. In the time since he'd proposed, he'd built a wheelchair ramp for Bobby and prepared a room for him. The doorways in the house had already been plenty wide. The bathroom would be a tight fit for the Hoyer lift, but Noah had plans in the works for a remodel. Acacia had said that there was a grant she could apply for once they were married. It would all work out.

He'd never known how good having a family would feel. He'd always felt he wanted one, but this feeling—this full, satisfied joy—was so unexpected. Every day when he woke, he recalled that Acacia loved him, and his love for her raced through him like a band of wild horses.

He squeezed her hand. They were in their final descent into Venice.

She opened her eyes, squinting to focus. "Are we there?"

"We are." He smiled into her beautiful brown eyes. He'd learned that Acacia was a Greek name meaning "everlasting", just as their love would be. How perfect it was.

Sitting up, she straightened the hem of her dress. "I can't wait to get to our hotel. The pictures were gorgeous. Thank you so much, Noah, for planning such a wonderful honeymoon for us."

"The travel planner gets all the credit. But I think the hotel's perfect, too." He slipped his arm around her shoulders and hugged her.

She lifted her lips for a kiss.

He cupped her face and captured her mouth, caressing her lips with his tongue, delving deep until she moaned softly. Nuzzling her neck, he slipped his fingers in her hair, sucked on her earlobe, and kissed her behind her ear. He whispered, "That hotel's going to be great for a lot of reasons."

They were near the front of the British Airways flight, so it didn't take them long to disembark. Once through customs, they headed outside to the arrivals area and searched for the hotel shuttle. They soon spotted the white van with *Hotel Ai Cavalieri di Venezia* written in beautiful script on the side. They hurried over, and Noah knocked on the window.

The driver hustled out. "Are you Signor Rowden?"

Noah reached out his hand. "Yes, and this is my wife, Acacia. Glad you were here waiting for us."

He shook Noah's hand. "And I am Piero. Welcome to Venice. Let me take your bags." Opening the van door, he said, "Please, get in."

Piero kept up a constant dialogue as he drove, describing the sights out the windows. Noah couldn't concentrate on his words. Instead, he anticipated everything the next few days would hold for them. It was late morning here in Venice, so they had plenty of time to drop their bags at the hotel and look around before dinner. Acacia was really looking forward to that.

And then there was tonight. His arm tightened around his new wife as his mind roamed over all the possibilities the night held. He leaned in and whispered in her ear, "I love you."

She turned and brushed a kiss across his lips. "I love you more."

His heart sped up. Yes, tonight would be full of wonderful possibilities.

When they stopped, he was surprised that they were in a small lot inside a cluster of many buildings, instead of in front of the hotel.

"This is Venice, my friends. From here we must walk. Come. I will bring the bags." Piero loaded their luggage on the waiting cart and they followed him around a corner and through a narrow walkway. When they came to a flight of concrete stairs, he said, "Please, continue down here. Turn right, and you will see the hotel entrance."

Noah held his arm at Acacia's waist as they descended. His body ached at the thought of taking her mouth in a deep kiss, and he almost did it despite the need to check in at their hotel. Instead, he gripped her waist and pulled her as close as possible to his taut body. The entrance was just a few feet past the steps, and the hotel was everything they'd hoped it would be.

Acacia sighed as they walked toward the large antique doors fronted with gorgeous potted trees. "Oh, Noah. Look at this. Isn't it wonderful? I can't believe we're staying here."

He smiled, enjoying her happiness. "It's beautiful."

As they entered the hotel lobby, they felt as though they were stepping back in time. Ornate antiques in quiet shades of blue and cream made up the décor.

A handsomely dressed clerk stood behind the marble front desk. "May I help you, signore?"

Noah took out his wallet and passport. "Reservations for Noah Rowden."

Acacia handed him her passport as well for the hotel to make a copy of.

"Sì, signore. You are expected."

Noah wrapped his arm around her, leaning down and planting a kiss on top of her head. God, she still smelled wonderful. Blood thrummed in his veins as he imagined the night to come.

In their room, the rich antique furnishings continued. An ornate chandelier hung from the arched ceiling and matching sconces flanked the large, sumptuous bed. Noah grinned at the sight of it. Two gold-trimmed closet doors meant adequate storage for all of the clothes Acacia had brought with her. A creamy velvet loveseat sat against one wall, while the other was a bank of windows overlooking the water. They'd be able to watch the canal traffic floating by from their room. The travel planner had done her job well.

Pulling Acacia into his arms, he looked deep into those gorgeous brown eyes. "I love you, baby. I'm glad you decided to marry me."

She stood on her tiptoes and caressed his neck, kissing him deeply and ending with a nip. "You've made me so happy, Noah. You're my miracle cowboy." Grinning up at him, she said, "I'm glad you asked me. Sometimes I think you wanted Bobby more than me."

He laughed. "Yeah, he was the dealmaker, all right." He grew solemn for a moment. "I hope he and Bobo are doing okay. I can't believe I'm already missing those two."

"I'll bet Bobby is doing just fine," Acacia replied. "He's the happiest person I know, and we both worked hard to prepare him for our absence."

He leaned in and claimed her lips like a starving man, twining his tongue with hers. Her body went soft in his arms. She undulated her hips against the aching bulge beneath his fly, and he bit back a groan. God, he wanted her. He pulled back and took a deep breath.

They both laughed and said, "I love you," at the same time.

She headed into the bathroom to change clothes, and his overactive imagination went with her as he changed in the bedroom. God, he was ready for this evening. At last, a room to themselves. There was nothing they had to do, nobody depending on them. It was a rare luxury.

Plopping down on the bed, he tested the softness and whether it squeaked. Oh yeah, the bed was just right. Tonight, with the beautiful woman who was about to walk out of that bathroom, would be one fantastic night.

Acacia opened the door, and he blew a low whistle. She looked sexy as hell in a short red dress and matching sandals.

With a curtsy, she said, "Why, thank you, cowboy."

Yes, he was a lucky man. As they left the room to go explore, he took a last look over his shoulder and grinned. Hot damn. Tonight was his honeymoon.

* * *

Acacia descended the thickly carpeted stairs from their second-floor room. Everything about their hotel was grand, from its marble floors to its frescoed ceilings. Noah kept his hand at her waist, protective as always. She was Cinderella at the palace with her prince—everything magical and perfect.

As they reached the bottom, he leaned down and kissed her. "How about we find some coffee, Mrs. Rowden?"

She grinned and patted his cheek. "I'd love that, husband. You lead the way."

Noah stopped at the front desk and asked directions to the nearest sidewalk café.

Out of the shade of the buildings, the temperature was perfect—in the mid-seventies. She looped her arm through Noah's as they walked. Europe was so different from the States. Everything here was ancient. It enchanted her to walk among buildings hundreds of years old that were still being used in everyday living. The pace was slower here as well. People strolled, rather than walked, pausing occasionally to chat or to take in their surroundings.

While stopped at a curb, waiting for traffic to clear, Noah pulled her into his embrace, capturing her lips in a passionate kiss. A sense of being cherished spread through her. People moved past them as she curled her arms around his neck and stood on her tiptoes, returning his kiss with an intensity of her own.

An old man passed them and chuckled quietly.

They arrived at the small café, and Noah seated her. A waiter came to take their order. Noah took her hand, and the love in his eyes sent tingles speeding through her. This time in Italy would be special. They'd waited so long to be alone, without responsibilities. Though she would miss Bobby, these seven days were theirs, and she would treasure every moment of them.

The waiter brought their croissants and coffee. Strong and black, the coffee needed plenty of cream. They watched pedestrians walk by, some obviously locals out on errands, others seeming to be tourists like themselves. Acacia felt the tension from the long flight drifting away with the slight breeze wafting down the sidewalk.

She reached across for Noah's hand, unable to stand the distance, even that of the small table, between them.

He smiled as if he understood her and felt the need pulling at him as well.

They were so in tune with one another now that it was hard to believe that they could have ever been so wrong about each other. Squeezing his hand, she whispered, "I love you, husband."

He grinned, the devil in his sparkling brown eyes. "I love you, wife, and I can't wait until tonight when I can show you just how much."

Laughing, she shook her head. "I may need some Red Bull. Do they sell that here?"

"We'll take time for a nap so you can recharge your batteries, my love. You won't need any Red Bull, I promise."

Noah summoned the waiter and paid the bill, and they set off walking again.

When they came to a magnificent bronze statue of a soldier on a horse, Noah took pictures of her standing in front of it. As she turned to look down the street, he came up behind her, wrapping his arms around her waist. As if he couldn't resist, he ran his lips down her neck so that she shivered. Kissing her ear, her neck, her jaw, he kept teasing her until goosebumps covered her arms.

Turning her around to face him, he caressed her lips with the tip of his tongue. She slid her arms around his neck, oblivious to her surroundings, and returned his kiss with an intensity of passion that let him know how much she wanted him.

He trailed his lips across her jaw and behind her ear, her favorite sensitive spot, and she sighed. "You always know what I want."

With a last, quick kiss, he released her. "Because I love you."

"And I'll love you forever, Noah."

Arm in arm, they continued down the sidewalk.

Later, Noah bought her a red rose from a vendor and handed it to her with a wry smile. "A token of my affections."

She sniffed its heady perfume and *aahed* in delight. "Thank you, love. I never get flowers."

"Well, I'll have to change that, won't I?"

His expression left her no doubt that he would.

The second time she covered a yawn, Noah said, "Let's go back to the hotel and take that nap. You'll need it before we go to dinner." Then he grinned. "And before tonight."

She laughed and clasped his arm tightly. "You crazy man."

It was a good thing Noah had paid attention to their winding path that afternoon, because she was completely turned around. But he led them unerringly back to their hotel. Once in the room, she curled up on the bed. All she needed now were the arms of her husband.

Noah climbed in beside her and pulled her against his chest. He kissed her forehead, her cheeks, and the tip of her nose. His hand caressed her belly and slid up to her breast, cupping it.

Sucking in a breath, she slipped her fingers through his, too sleepy to do more than smile.

Sighing, he said, "Sleep well, darling."

Had anything ever felt this good? His heart beat quietly in her ear. Safe and warm, she slid her leg between his and closed her eyes. This was her man, forever and ever now. Her life couldn't be more perfect.

#

She awoke to Noah's deep breathing. Poor thing, he was sleeping hard. Slipping out of bed, she gathered her shower paraphernalia and headed for the bathroom.

Later, as she towel-dried her hair, she heard Noah moving about the room. Good, he was awake. Her heart kicked up its beat in anticipation of seeing her handsome husband. She'd move in there in a few minutes and let him have the shower.

When she opened the door, Noah stood at the bed, clad only in his jeans. His bare upper half drew her gaze like a magnet. His muscular chest and washboard abs didn't come from working out, but from working with patients all day and handling livestock and roping on the weekends. His was a working man's body. And it made her drool.

He must have noticed because he grinned and spread his arms.

She practically flew to his embrace. Would she ever get enough of him? Lifting her face for his kiss, she knew the answer. She'd never have enough. Never. Kissing him hungrily, she didn't want to let him go.

He crab-walked her to the wall and pushed her up against it, linking their fingers and raising her hands above her head.

Helpless and loving it, she nipped his lip and thrust her tongue deep into his mouth, caressing him.

Noah moaned and pressed his hips into her, murmuring, "We'd better stop, or we'll never make our dinner reservations."

She giggled as he pulled back, noticing the warm tide of lust in his eyes.

"Well, I'm hungry, so we can't do that," she said.

He picked up his shaving kit from the bed and headed for the bathroom. Casting a glance back at her, he said, "Woman, you'll kill me one of these days."

She grinned saucily at him.

She was dressed in her bathrobe but nearly ready when he came out. Seeing him wrapped in a towel and smelling like the man she loved, it was all she could do to stay seated. If they were going to eat dinner, she'd better head to the bathroom to finish her hair and get dressed.

Tonight, she was wearing a black strapless evening dress with a tight bodice that pushed up her breasts nicely. The skirt flared at the hips and ended six inches above the knee. The outfit was sexy and retro, and she felt amazing in it.

When she came out, Noah turned and his mouth opened in an "O" of appreciation. He held out his hand and she came to him. Tilting her chin, he said softly. "You look so, so lovely tonight, honey." And he kissed her.

This really was like Cinderella.

Noah was dressed and ready to go, and, God, he was gorgeous. His gray dress shirt tucked neatly into his starched Wranglers set off his broad shoulders magnificently. Those lean hips, fitted so well by the jeans, gave her all sorts of ideas about the evening to come. His trophy buckle shone in the light. Her miracle cowboy was an awesome sight. She patted his cheek. "You handsome thing. Those Italian women better keep their hands off you tonight."

He threw his head back and laughed. "I'm all yours. I promise." Taking her hand, he led her out the door.

* * *

All through dinner at L'Osteria di Santa Marina, her thoughts turned to the night ahead. Alone at last with Noah, in the beautiful hotel, far away from responsibilities and interruptions, a fantastical evening awaited. Noah kept eyeing her, and she knew his thoughts were on the same kinds of things. She ran the toe of her four-inch heel up his leg, and he grinned. Raising her brows, she set her lips in a sexy pout. Slipping off her shoe, she slid her bare foot up his calf, going farther, nestling her toes against his now prominent erection.

He bit back a grin, pressed his lips together, and rolled his eyes.

She slid the ball of her foot up and down his zipper. She could tell by his rounded eyes that she was driving him wild.

Grabbing the edge of the table, he groaned.

She giggled and lowered her foot.

He shook his head and mouthed, "I love you."

Dinner was wonderful, and she had two glasses of wine. In all honesty, the food could have been mediocre, and she wouldn't have noticed. Noah was her focus. Every word, every movement of his captured her attention. This was the man she loved, and he was finally, finally hers. This night was perfect in every way just because he was with her.

Noah paid the bill and helped her from her chair. He slid his arm around her, and a wild thrill rushed through her body. It was time. Her honeymoon night was beginning.

As they walked arm in arm through the dimly lit streets and alleyways, she grew more focused. His hip, higher than hers, rubbed against her. His smell, masculine yet a little sweet, wafted down to her. His fingers brushed up and down her arm in a caress.

They detoured down to the canal, its evening lights and romantic setting a perfect ending to this first day in Venice.

Noah pulled her into a darkened doorway and locked eyes with her. Her lips parted with surprise, and he leaned in for a kiss. It started as seductive, slowly inflaming, but the sighing sound she made must have driven him over the edge, and he took her mouth with hungry strokes of his tongue. She wound her fingers through his hair, scraped them down his chest and abdomen, and then tucked them into his jeans. He pressed her hips against the wall, his erection hard against her.

She breathed in his passion, giving him back her own, clasping his neck and thrusting her tongue into his mouth. She wanted him so badly—this man whose slightest touch sent her pulse racing.

He caressed her breast, finding her sensitive nipple, sweeping soft kisses up her jaw, and nibbling behind her ear.

The man was driving her wild. She wrapped her leg around him, clutched his shoulders and kissed him for all she was worth, mumbling when she came up for air, "Get me to that room, now, or I'll make a spectacle of myself."

Laughing wildly, he slipped his arm around her waist. "As much as I'd like to see that, I don't want to spend my wedding night in a cell. Come on, you."

She leaned her head into him while they walked. This man loved her. She still, sometimes, couldn't believe it.

They turned into the hotel entrance, and he dropped his arm to hold her hand.

The clerk greeted them as they walked by. "*Buonanotte*, signore, signora."

They spoke in unison. "Good night."

* * *

She dropped her evening bag on the bed and turned to Noah.

He rested his hands on her hips and eased her toward him, a devilish look in his eyes. "Mrs. Rowden, I give you first dibs on the bathroom."

Her heart sped up. "Well, you better let me go then, cowboy."

He growled. "Not without a kiss, I won't."

She rose up on her tiptoes and gave him a quick smack on the lips.

"You call that a kiss?" His voice was a husky rasp that sent shivers down her spine.

"If I give you any more, I won't make it to the bathroom."

He slapped her bottom and let her go.

She grinned, loving it, sure it would be the first of many pops on the rear end he'd give her.

When she came out in the short black negligée she'd bought for the night, he gusted out a breath and headed straight for her. "Now, this is what I'm talking about, wife. You sure are sexy." He backed her up against the wall and kissed her, making it last until she giggled and pulled back.

"Would you get on into the bathroom so we can get this show on the road?"

He laughed. "Well, if you put it like that..." Already down to his jeans, he headed for the bathroom with his kit.

She folded the thick duvet at the foot of the bed, then drew the sheets down. Peeking through the gap in the window curtains, she watched a gondola float by with a couple sitting close together on the seat. She and Noah were taking a gondola ride tomorrow on the Grand Canal. The following day, they'd head to Rome. She couldn't wait to see all of the sights there. What a fabulous honeymoon Noah had planned.

The door opened, and he came out. Watching her with heated eyes, he unfastened his Wranglers and lowered the zipper.

She walked around the bed and pulled him down for a long kiss. The taste of his clean mouth was heavenly, inviting her to explore. Releasing him, she smiled into his eyes. "I love you, husband."

He pulled her toward the bed, his eyes devouring every inch of her. "Climb in here, and you can show me how much."

She slipped under the covers and moved over, making room for him.

He dropped his Wranglers and briefs, and his erection sprang up.

Sliding in beside her, he took her in his arms, leaning above her. "I love you, Acacia. I promise I always will."

Her chest tightened. "I'll love you forever, Noah." She needed his touch, his desire, his love. She craned her head toward him, and he smiled. He must know what she needed.

Her mouth opened beneath the pressure of his lips, and she welcomed his tongue as it stroked hers, teasing her, stirring her senses and nerves so that she was hot and molten like a horseshoe in a blacksmith's hand. She was pure liquid by the time Noah ended the kiss.

He pushed up and looked down at her, gently brushing her hair back from her forehead. "You're so beautiful, Acacia. I'll never get over feeling lucky you're mine."

"I'm the lucky one. I never thought I'd find a man who would love me knowing that I had Bobby in my life. You're the special one, Noah." She grinned. "Oh, and you might be a little gorgeous yourself, too."

He kissed her again, slowly, taking his time. Languid warmth turned into fire. His calloused palm slid up the outside of her leg, paused at her hip, and reached behind her to squeeze her rear, making need burst through her body. He slipped his hand over her hip and down to her pelvis. Daring fingertips slipped into her panties.

She pulled his hips closer, feeling his hardness. He pushed against her, and she raised her pelvis toward him, her pulse racing. His fingers were doing diabolical things to her.

He slid his lips to her neck and nuzzled her, landing soft kisses down toward her breasts. He stopped at the low-cut lace of her gown. "I think it's time to remove this, don't you?"

She sat up, her pulse running full throttle. "High time, husband."

He helped her slip it off and tossed it on the floor. Then he removed her panties. When she moved to lie down, he held her up, admiring her. "God, you're lovely." He cupped her breast, rubbing his thumb across her nipple.

Her breath caught as a hot spurt of desire shot through her.

He smiled and laid her on her back, his head dipping to suckle her breast. Her hips lifted, arching against him as the warm wet tugs on her nipple made everything inside her tighten and ache.

He raised up, looking down at her with a satisfied grin.

Oh, yes, he was pleasing her all right. And she loved that he was hers, that she got to see him this way, so open and hungry and sexy as hell.

Raising up, she caught his beautifully etched mouth in a kiss. "I love you, Noah."

He looked into her eyes, serious this time. "And, I love you, with my heart and soul, Acacia."

His fervent declaration reverberated through her. A woman could wait a lifetime to hear those words. Tears pooled in her eyes and she pulled him down to her, brushing her lips against his, kissing him softly, cradling his face in her hands. "You're everything I've ever dreamed of, and more than I ever thought I'd have."

Nuzzling her neck, he whispered in her ear, "Let me love you now."

She nodded, "Please, Noah, love me."

He lowered his head, kissing until he found her breast. She hissed as he circled her nipple with his tongue, suckling it until it pebbled hard in his mouth. Waves of pleasure washed through her. He reached between her legs, his fingers delving reverently into her cleft. The roughened pads stroked over her sensitive place and skirted the opening to her core. He kissed her mouth, exploring her with his tongue. She moaned, her hips circling. He fingered her leisurely, building her need, his kiss a slow, deep mimic of penetration. Her heels dug into the bed as she pushed into the movement.

She couldn't breathe for the pleasure, her entire body quivering as he cupped her in his hand and his finger slid into her. His palm rubbed against her, his fingertip stroking over delicate tissues. His other hand gripped her hip, holding her in place, restraining her.

She reached out and took him in her hand, gripping him firmly. He groaned, and she pushed him back so that he lay on the bed. He was hard, and she pumped him from root to tip. He leaned back against the headboard with a groan. This was what she wanted—to pleasure him. She stroked him until he grabbed her hand, forcing her to stop, a dazed and lustful expression blazing from his eyes.

He pushed her back on the bed and kissed her hard, hungrily. She welcomed his fierceness. She wanted him just as much. Reaching for him, she guided him to her. He stared into her eyes, his love all but overwhelming her. She wanted him inside her, wanted all of him, everything he could give her. She arched up, and he pushed in. He felt too big, although she was wet as hell.

Noah groaned and threw back his head. "God, Acacia, you feel good. You tell me what you want, okay?" He looked at her and waited. "Okay?"

"I want you, like this, right now. Don't stop."

He laughed and moved inside her, slowly at first.

She ran her hands along the strong muscles of his back as pleasure grew inside her. He was moving faster now, the muscles of his butt flexing hard. She loved the feel of them.

Then he slowed and came to a stop.

She asked, "Something wrong?"

He pulled out and grinned. "Oh, *hell* no." He leaned down to give her a long, leisurely kiss on the lips, then moved to her neck and down to her breast as jolts of electricity sang through her. Would the man ever quit torturing her? He nibbled his way down her tummy, sending shivers up her spine.

"I love you," he said. Now at her thighs, he kissed each one. She gasped at the dizzying spiral of sensation his touch produced as he traced upward with his tongue. Her core clenched in near painful need. He lifted her hips, opening her to him. She moaned, anticipating what would come next.

With each stroke of Noah's tongue, Acacia sank deeper into the sensations he created in her. She trembled, on the edge, arching up as her desire burned hotter and hotter.

Pleasure concentrated low and deep. Colors of the Venetian glass they'd seen swirled behind her eyes. Her world spun out of control, making her blood pound and her heart race. Panting, she groaned as his tongue moved inside her. His touch, the heat of his mouth, the sound of his voice, drove her to ecstasy.

She lost contact with the here and now. Noah's touch became unbearable. She shattered, rising into the heavens on wings of fire.

A moment later, Noah rose and pulled her over on top of him, holding her close. She opened her eyes, needing something more. Straddling him, she guided him inside.

His eyes opened wide and he grinned up at her. "Now?"

"Right now!" she answered, and ground herself down on him.

He groaned and grabbed her hips, sliding her back and forth in rhythm with her own thrusts. She leaned backward and clutched his thighs, arching her back and continuing to rock.

Noah groaned again. "Oh, God, like that, Acacia."

And she had a lifetime of these nights ahead of her? Seconds later, she leaned forward, capturing his mouth, kissing him hard.

He cupped her neck and raked her with his tongue, claiming her for his own. Grabbing her hips, he flipped her on her back. Still connected, he pumped into her, first gently, then harder.

She grabbed him, pulling him into her until his hips slapped against her. "Harder, Noah. I love you. Harder!"

He grinned, love and lust rampant in his eyes, and upped his game. Bliss washed through her, taking her up and up, almost to the brink again. She wrapped her legs around him.

Noah threw his head back and called her name, and she was there again, pleasure rupturing her sanity. He plunged into her one last time, spilling into her in a hot flood.

Soon they lay spent, Noah with his arm thrown across her. It took minutes for her heart to slow. Never had making love been so fulfilling, so amazing.

Noah opened an eye and raised his brow. "I want a drink of water, but I don't think I can walk."

She groaned. "Ditto. You wore me out."

He cracked up. "Well, since you're thirsty too, I'll make the effort."

He walked to the bathroom naked and without a hint of embarrassment while she admired the view.

He strode back over with the water and got under the covers. "Drink up. You need to stay hydrated." The grin he gave her left no doubt as to his intentions.

She drank, then snuggled against his chest, warm and safe and satisfied.

He kissed her gently.

This was her life now. She had her miracle cowboy. God really did answer prayers.

EPILOGUE

Acacia finished changing two-month-old Becca's diaper. They'd named the baby after Acacia's mother, Rebecca, who they'd lost last year to the breast cancer she'd fought for so long and so hard.

Noah would be home from work soon. Acacia liked getting outside each day, so she'd taken Becca down in the stroller and fed the stock. Bobby, now more independent in his electric wheelchair, had followed along beside her. Noah had told her that she didn't have to feed the stock, but he was already working harder. He'd taken on extra clients, trying to set aside more funds to start his own PT business, and feeding was the least she could do for him.

While she was alone and caring for Bobby, going back to nursing had seemed so important, as if it was the only way to get her independence back. Now that she was married to Noah, and especially since she'd become Becca's mother, that goal held less meaning for her.

The change in her outlook had surprised her at first, even though she'd always imagined herself as a ranch wife and a mother. But a nursing career had always been a part of that imagined future.

She loved making a home for Noah, and being a mother fulfilled her in ways that she'd never dreamed of. She couldn't imagine a more amazing life than the one she was living now.

Bobby, happy as ever, adored his niece. And he loved helping with her. He'd come a long way in his therapy, gaining more and more control over his arms. Learning to use his new wheelchair was just the beginning. All thanks to Noah.

The diesel engine of Noah's truck sounded in the driveway. Her heart sped up. Even three years after their wedding, she still couldn't wait to see him.

She opened the door as he walked up onto the front porch. "Howdy, stranger."

He grinned. "Howdy, gorgeous."

He came in and dropped his therapy bag by the door, giving her a quick kiss on the cheek and taking his daughter from her. "Now, who is this pretty little thing?"

Becca stared at him with her dark-blue eyes, making wet, drooling sounds.

"That's right. It's Daddy. You know me." He lifted her in the air and made funny faces at her, then pulled her in for a kiss.

"Hi, Noah," Bobby called. Bobo, as always, lay sleeping at the foot of his master's wheelchair.

Noah tucked Becca into the crook of his arm and walked over to him. "Hey, buddy. How was your day?"

"Good. Will you play with me?"

Noah laughed. "No rest for the wicked, huh?"

"You always say that, Noah."

"I'll make a deal with you, buddy. You hold my daughter while I love on my wife, and I'll take you out to see Mini in the horse pasture. It's about time Becca met your mini horse, don't you think?"

Bobby grinned. "Yay! Okay, I like Becca."

Noah settled the baby in the crook of Bobby's arm, pulling it snugly against her. "Sit just like that."

"Okay, Noah."

He turned to Acacia and opened his arms. "Come here, you. It's been a long day and I need some lovin' from my wife."

She caught her breath—then ran to him. Noah, her miracle cowboy, set her heart on fire.

SNEAK PEEK - THE LASSOED HEARTS SERIES

THE COWBOY'S COVER GIRL

Knox McGinnis removed the halter from his big bay gelding and swatted him on the rump. The horse trotted off into the wheat pasture, seemingly unaffected by the long day sorting cattle on the 11,200-acre McGinnis ranch near the tiny town of Rule in north Texas. So close to west Texas that it shared the wild, desert landscape, the McGinnis property had its share of mesquite trees and prickly pear cactus. But the hardy natural grasses grew healthy white-tailed deer for the hunters that the ranch hosted each year and robust black angus cattle that were his father's pride.

After returning the halter to the big metal barn, he paused before entering the ranch house. His sister Jessica's SUV was parked out front which meant that she was back from the airport in Abilene. Should he head into Haskell for dinner? Meeting some stranger from New York wasn't high on his list after a hard day in the saddle. But what he really wanted was a shower and to hit the sack early. Better go in and get it over with.

As soon as he entered the big kitchen where everyone was already seated at the table, he locked eyes with Jessica's friend. Gritting his teeth, he steeled himself to show no reaction at her revealing outfit, a lime-green satin jacket over a black crocheted top with holes easily two inches wide clearly showing her tiny beige bra underneath. Is that what went for acceptable fashion in New York? He slid his glance away and headed to the sink to wash his hands.

When he took his seat at the table, Jessica spoke up. "Hey, brother, I'd like you to meet my friend, Sadie Stewart. Sadie, this is my big brother, Knox."

Keeping his face neutral out of respect for his baby sister, he nodded. "Pleased to meet you, ma'am."

Sadie raised her eyebrows. "I'm only twenty-six. Am I a ma'am already?"

He didn't look at her, instead serving himself a steak. "In Texas all women are ma'am."

"Well, isn't that nice."

But she didn't sound like she thought it was nice. She sounded condescending. Who did she think she was? He served himself from the rest of the dishes without comment, already taking a healthy dislike to the northerner. He took a bite of his fried potatoes and noticed that she only had a plate of salad in front of her. What the hell? Was she too good for his family's country food? He glanced up and noticed Jessica watching him.

"Sadie's a vegetarian," she said.

He stifled a groan. Of course she was. He didn't acknowledge his sister's comment, taking a bite of green beans instead.

"Don't they have good black angus steaks in New York, Sadie?" his dad asked.

Sadie smiled. "I'm sure they do, Jeb. I just don't eat them."

"No wonder you're so skinny. A person could get sickly going without good beef," his father replied with a smile.

She obviously didn't take his comment personally because she returned his dad's smile. "I get plenty of protein, Jeb, I just don't eat animals in the process."

Knox restrained himself from rolling his eyes and took a quick bite of potatoes. This city-slicker was going to get on his nerves every time she opened her mouth, and the sooner he left the table the better.

Maddie, Knox's mom, and always the peacemaker in the house, spoke up. "To each his own, I say. Sadie, I have to get groceries in Abilene this week. Why don't you come with me and we'll make sure you have plenty of meal choices from now on, okay?"

"That sounds wonderful, Maddie. Thank you." She looked genuinely appreciative and this appeased Knox some. But still. A vegetarian? Come on.

"So, how was your flight, Sadie?" his mother asked.

"It was fine. I guess I do so much of it that I don't pay much attention to flying anymore. The only thing that got my pulse racing was a tight time frame for my plane switch in Dallas. The little commuter I took to Abilene wasn't crowded, though, so that was nice."

"Well, we're sure glad you got here safely," his mom replied.

"It's great to be here, Maggie. Thanks so much for having me. This is a beautiful place. I've heard so much about Texas, and I can't wait to see a real working cattle ranch."

He pressed his lips together. *Damn.* That didn't sound good. Did Jessica have plans for the two of them to follow him around?

"Sadie and I'll do the clean-up after dinner, mom," Jessica offered.

Sadie's head bobbed up and her eyes widened in surprise.

He grimaced. What? Was she too good to do some dishes?

"Um, do you have gloves?" Sadie asked.

"I don't think so, but we can get some. You can dry tonight," his sister answered.

Sadie smiled. "That sounds perfect."

Well, he had to give it to her. She'd taken that in stride. Maybe there was more to the woman than met the eyes. He finished the last of his food and went to the sink to rinse off his plate.

"It was nice meeting you, Knox."

He put his plate in the dishwasher before replying. "Welcome to the McGinnis Ranch, Miss Stewart."

"Oh, call me Sadie, please."

He nodded. "Good evening, Sadie." He strode from the room, wondering just how long the strange woman from New York City would be staying.

* * *

Sadie finished drying the plate and stacked it in the overhead cabinet with the others. There was surprising comfort in this everyday task. In her flat in the city, she had a maid who took care of chores like this and who dropped off and picked up her cleaning among a variety of other chores that made Sadie's life easier. With her annual modeling salary in the millions, there wasn't much in life that she couldn't pay for and skimping on staff and necessities was something she never did.

As one of the world's top supermodels, her life was incredibly fast paced. It took everything from her. She'd become jaded with the world, burnt out with the fashion industry, with the back-stabbing and hateful gossip, and the constant travel and being on display every moment. That was the reason she'd sought refuge here with Jessica on her isolated Texas ranch.

In the past months, life had lost its meaning, food its appeal. When she'd fainted in the middle of a shoot, she'd realized that she'd reached her breaking point. She'd called Jessica and asked if she could come to Texas.

And what an unlikely pair they were. They'd met while Jessica was studying art at NYU and working in a coffee shop. Sadie had come in, stressed and out of sorts. Jessica's sunny disposition and natural kindness had breached Sadie's black mood and over the next few weeks, they'd become friends.

She and Jessica had stayed in touch after she'd moved back to Texas, facetiming and texting several times a week. Sadie had come to lean on her pragmatic, down-to-earth friend for advice and a sane voice in the chaos of her world-traveling life.

Jessica handed Sadie the last bowl. "How about we go outside? I'll show you around the place."

"I'd like that."

A few moments later, they stood at the pasture fence where a small herd of horses grazed. Jessica pointed to a sorrel mare. "That one there, the one that's kind of orangey red? She's mine."

"She's beautiful. What breed is she?"

"We have Quarter Horses here on the ranch. They're the most suited to working with cattle. Would you like me to catch her up? We could brush her. She loves that."

"Oh, that would be wonderful!" Sadie looked down at her heels. "I'm not really dressed for this, am I?"

Jessica grinned. "Not at all. Do you want to change first?"

That would take time. Did it really matter? She didn't have much in the way of ranch clothes in her wardrobe, and she'd been so exhausted before she came that she hadn't been able to face going shopping. "No, I'm fine like this."

"Just don't get stepped on with those pretty pink-painted toenails sticking out of your shoes."

Soon the mare was tied in the barn and Jessica handed Sadie a brush. "Look at the way the hair grows and brush in that direction. She'll love it."

Sadie examined the mare's back and made her first stoke as Jessica moved to the horse's other side to work. Soon, she had a rhythm going with her strokes and the mare's head lowered. She was obviously loving the attention. Sadie stopped and moved to her beautiful head, petting the round, muscular cheek and looking into the mare's large brown eyes. The mare's calm gaze soothed Sadie's soul. She kissed her muzzle, smelling the fresh grass on the mare's breath. Sadie closed her eyes and inhaled again. This is what life should be about.

Footsteps sounded at the barn entrance and she opened her eyes. Knox strode into the barn, a rifle on his arm, his eyes taking in the sight of her holding the horse's head in her hands. He glanced away and moved to the shelves on the wall.

"What's up, brother?" Jessica asked.

"Got to dart a bull in the morning."

"Really? What's going on?

Sadie listened attentively, her eyes never leaving his hands as he pulled medicine from the fridge and loaded a dart.

"Vet's coming in the morning. Bull's got an abscess. He's hell to load without trancing him." He capped the dart and stuck it in his shirt pocket.

She couldn't take her eyes from him. His economical movements spoke of long practice. He was so self-assured.

Jessica headed for the tack room and a few seconds later, called out, "I can't find a hoof pick."

Knox let out a long sigh and headed that way.

Sadie grinned. That was so like a big brother.

Jessica came out brandishing the pick. "Can't bring a horse in without cleaning its hooves."

Knox returned to the workbench and the rifle.

Sadie stared at him. What makes this man tick? Why is he so reticent? Men usually stared at her. Wanted to talk to her. He wouldn't even look at her. It felt odd. He didn't seem like the shy type. He just appeared uninterested and for some reason that bothered her.

Jessica looked up, "Have you ridden before, Sadie?"

She smiled lopsidedly. "I don't know if you'd call it riding. I had a perfume photoshoot where I had to climb on a huge Saddlebred horse. He was beautiful but was really nervous with everything going on around us. All I knew about riding was what the owner told me right before he boosted me up into the little saddle. The guy showed me how to hold the reins and then I was on my own. The poor horse kept shying off every time the camera clicked. I was supposed to look accomplished and carefree in my spiffy riding outfit."

"Oh, Lord. How did you keep from falling off?" Jessica asked.

Sadie glanced at Knox and could tell that he was following the conversation. "I wasn't about to fall off. It was an important shoot. I just pretended to be someone else, someone who knew how to ride, and I got through the afternoon just fine."

Jessica raised her brows. "That's a neat trick."

Sadie smiled. "I have to use it from time to time when photographers spring crazy things on me."

As Jessica cleaned the mare's hooves, she asked, "Can we go with you tomorrow, Knox? I'm sure Sadie would love to watch you work cattle."

His glance slid to Sadie, then away. Putting the vial of tranquilizer back into the fridge, he kept silent. Finally, on his way out of the barn, he said, "Suit yourselves."

Jessica rolled her eyes and grinned at Sadie. "A man of few words, my brother."

Sadie sighed. "I don't think he likes me."

"Don't worry about it. He's a pretty serious guy. I'm sure most people find him pretty hard to get to know." She untied the mare. "Let's turn her out and get back to the house."

Sadie's gaze slid outside to where Knox stood at his truck. The handsome cowboy was an enigma. She inspected his fine-looking butt. And a man she might want to get to know.

KEEP READING FOR A FREE BOOK OFFER!

GET YOUR FREE BOOK

www.janalynknight.com

ALSO BY JANALYN KNIGHT

Cowboy for a Season
True Blue Texas Cowboy
The Govain Cowboys Series
The Cowboy's Fate
The Cowboy's Choice
The Cowboy's Wish
The Howelton Texas Series
Cowboy Refuge
Cowboy Promise
Cowboy Strong
The Tough Texan Series
Stone One Tough Texan
North Their Tough Texan
Clint Her Tough Texan
The Cowboy SEALs Series
The Cowboy SEAL's Secret Baby
The Cowboy SEAL's Daddy School
The Cowboy SEAL'S Second Chance
The Texas Knight Series
Her Guardian Angel Cowboy
Her Ride or Die Cowboy
Her Miracle Cowboy
Find your next handsome hunk now at:
Janalyn Knight books on Amazon

DEAR READER

Thank you so much for reading my books. Drop by my website at www.janalynknight.com[1] and join my *Wranglers Readers Group* to be the first to get a look at my newest books and to enter my many giveaways. Or, if you like leaving reviews of the books you read, become a member of my *POSSE Review Team* at Join my POSSE[2] page on my website at www.janalynknight.com[3] and get advance copies of my new books in exchange for leaving honest reviews.

You can also talk to me on Facebook[4] at Facebook.com/janalynknight

Follow me on BookBub by searching for Janalyn Knight in authors and get a New Release Alert when my next book comes out.

Follow me on Twitter with @Janalyn_Knight and be the first to find out when my books are on sale.

Follow me on Instagram with janalynknight where you'll see some of the amazing horses from the refuge where I volunteer

Until next time, may all your dreams be of cowboys!

Janalyn Knight

---

1. http://www.janalynknight.com

2. https://janalynknight.com/join-my-posse/

3. http://www.janalynknight.com

4. https://www.facebook.com/janalynknight

If you enjoyed Noah's book, please leave a review. Reviews are the life's-blood of an author's living and are very much appreciated!

REVIEW HER MIRACLE COWBOY ON AMAZON

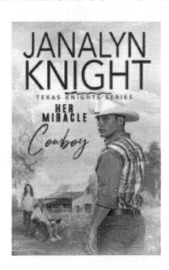

COPYRIGHT

About the Author

Nobody knows sexy Texas cowboys like Janalyn. From an early age, she competed in rodeo, later working on a ten-thousand-acre cattle ranch, and these experiences lend an authenticity to her characters and stories. Janalyn is an avid supporter of the Brighter Days Horse Refuge and totally owns the title of wine drinker extraordinaire. When she's not writing spicy cowboy romances, she's living her dream—sharing her twenty-acres of Texas Hill Country with her daughters and their families.

Read more at https://janalynknight.com/.

Made in the USA
Las Vegas, NV
15 January 2022

41492138R00129